BALLET SHOES FOR ANNA

Noel Streatfeild was born on Christmas Eve in 1885. She was the second daughter of the Bishop of Lewes, and grew up a strong-willed and difficult child (a story she tells in *A Vicarage Family*). From an early age she was determined to become an actor, and indeed attended the Academy of Dramatic Art, before performing for nine years in the West End and abroad.

It was a sudden decision to become an author, and at first she wrote only for adults. In 1936, however, she wrote *Ballet Shoes*, her most famous book, and two years later won the prestigious Carnegie Medal for *The Circus is Coming*. She then planned to write children's and adult novels alternately, but her success as a children's author made this impossible.

Although Noel had no children herself, she never failed to supply the kind of book that children wanted to read. She put this down to the fact that she could remember very vividly being a child herself, and that she had a "blotting-paper memory"!

by the same author

Ballet Shoes
The Gemma Series
White Boots
A Vicarage Family
Apple Bough
The Painted Garden
When the Siren Wailed
Thursday's Child
Far to Go
Tennis Shoes
The Circus is Coming
Party Frock

Collins Modern Classics

Ballet Shoes for Anna

by

Noel Streatfeild

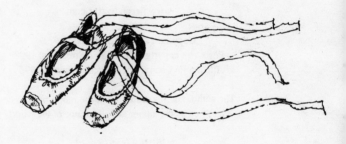

Illustrated by Victor Ambrus

Collins
An imprint of HarperCollinsPublishers

First published in Great Britain by William Collins Sons & Co. Ltd 1972
First published as a Collins Modern Classics 1998

3 5 7 9 11 10 8 6 4 2

Collins Modern Classics is an imprint of
HarperCollins*Publishers* Ltd, 77-85 Fulham Palace Road,
Hammersmith, London W6 8JB

The HarperCollins website address is
www.**fire**and**water**.com

ISBN 0 00 675398 1

Printed and bound in Great Britain by
Caledonian International Book Manufacturing Ltd,
Glasgow G64

CONTENTS

For Jeremy, Bridget and Andrew Brooke
Third Generation Rhodesians

Darlings,
I learnt what it was like to live through an earthquake
sitting on your granny's verandah in Rhodesia. So I
thought this book belonged especially to you.

Love,
NOEL

Prologue

ANNA SAT ON the caravan steps. She was dressed for her dancing lesson in a white tunic. She was tying on her pink dancing slippers. When the shoes were on she glanced up and saw what she thought was something extraordinary. It was birds, hundreds, perhaps thousands of them, all collecting on the hill above the village. Living in a caravan, Anna was always travelling so she accepted that in Turkey, where she now was, birds perhaps behaved differently from birds in other countries. For in her experience when birds migrated it was never in the very middle of summer, yet migrate was what these birds were clearly going to do. There was the usual bustle and excitement migrating birds always seemed to create. Then suddenly, as if someone had fired a starting pistol for a race, the birds took to the air and, looking like a black cloud, flew away. Not a bird stayed behind – not a single one.

Never at her dancing lessons with her grandfather did Anna let her mind wander. The lessons were held in the main room of Jardek's little white cottage. Against one wall he had put up a barre made and polished by himself. Always lessons started the same way. Jardek would say "Demi-plié, Anna. Twelve very beautiful."

That day, though she tried not to think about it, at the back of Anna's mind was a question: Why did the birds fly away?

After her lesson Anna went back to the caravan. She stood on the steps and gazed in all directions. Nowhere, on the ground, in the trees, on the roofs or in the air was one bird. Not a bird anywhere.

1. The Story Begins

TO THE CHILDREN Grandfather and Grandmother's little house in Turkey was home. This was because it was the only proper house they ever stayed in.

Francesco, the eldest of the three children, had said to his grandmother:

"It is so good that you never move anything. Always we know when we stay with you that all will be as we left it."

Augustus, the second boy, who was known as Gussie, had agreed fervently – Gussie was often fervent.

"Nothing, absolutely nothing, can be more beautiful than that."

Anna was the youngest. She added softly:

"Nothing – nothing ever."

The children did not call their grandparents Grandfather and Grandmother because they were the father and mother of their mother Olga who was Polish. Instead they called them Jardek and Babka. This was not the proper spelling but it was how the words sounded to the children. They had never seen them written down.

The children were British because that was what their father was, but they had never been to England. Their father was an artist called Christopher Docksay. Even when he was quite small it was clear that Christopher was meant to be an artist; but his father refused to admit this, hoping that if he ignored the child's talent it would die out of him. Mr Docksay worked in a bank and it was his ambition to become a bank manager. He thought being a bank manager was a splendid secure life so he wanted his sons, Cecil and Christopher, to grow up to be bank managers too.

Cecil was very like his father so he agreed with him that the best career in the world was to work in a bank. At school he studied hard — especially at mathematics — which he thought would help him to become a bank manager, and as soon as he was old enough he left school and joined a bank. Christopher, who was many years younger than Cecil, hardly worked at his lessons at all, spending much time filling his exercise books with drawings, and when he should have been doing his homework he was painting.

The teachers at the school where Christopher went of course knew all about his wanting to be an artist, and the headmaster did his best to get the boy's father to allow him to try for a scholarship to an art school.

"Your son has real talent, Mr Docksay, he should be given

his chance. I'm sure he'd win a scholarship."

But Mr Docksay would not listen. He made a noise like a horse makes when he gets chaff up his nose.

"Art! Nonsense! No future in it!"

Then one day when he was fifteen, Christopher decided he could bear life no longer. He must find someone to teach him to paint and he must live amongst painters. He searched the house for things that would sell, then he flew away to Paris. That, as far as his mother and father were concerned, was that, for he never heard from them again. But he did try. For the first two years after he had run away he drew what he thought were very funny pictures of himself on Christmas cards and sent them home, but he got no answer though he was careful to give his address.

"I suppose they're still sulking about the few bits and pieces I took, to pay my fare to Paris," Christopher grumbled to his friends, "but they shouldn't, the old man can put it against anything he may be going to leave me in his will."

Christopher had a very hard time in Paris and often he nearly starved, but he achieved his ambition. He became not only an artist but also a very good one. He had a rare gift for getting on to canvas light and heat such as you see and feel in hot countries. So by degrees his name became known and his pictures sold.

In order to paint the sort of pictures he liked painting Christopher was always moving about. He believed in being mobile so he bought an old gypsy caravan and a piebald horse called Togo and for many years drove wherever the mood took him. In those days he thought himself the luckiest fellow in the world. But that was before he drove into the little village in Turkey where he learnt what real happiness could be.

It was a very tumbledown little village on the side of a hill – just a few whitewashed cottages with their roofs held down by strong branches cut from trees, for the wind could be so savage it could blow the roofs off. There was also a shop, a very small mosque and a tea house. But what made Christopher pull Togo up outside the smallest of the cottages was the light. For some reason it shimmered and danced on that village in a way he had not seen before, and the cottages threw back the heat so violently it was as if it had substance so could be touched. Then, while he was gazing at the effects of heat and light, the door of the cottage outside which the caravan was standing opened and out came what Christopher thought was the loveliest girl he had ever seen. She was Olga.

Naturally, after seeing Olga together with the glorious light on the village, Christopher decided to stay. He made an arrangement for Togo to share a field with some cows, parked his caravan on the side of the road and settled down for a visit which should last until Olga agreed to marry him, which he knew might take time. Why should Olga wish to marry a man so much older than herself?

The marriage happened six months later. That was when, if the children were about when the story was being told, they would join in.

"One year after that when we are in Iran I was born," Francesco would say.

Then Gussie would burst out:

"I was born farthest away. I was born in India."

"Only just," his mother would say, smiling at Christopher. "One more day and you would have been born in Pakistan, but you were in such a hurry to arrive."

Anna knew she was the lucky one.

"Me, I was born in Turkey staying with Jardek and Babka, so I was the only one not born in our caravan."

Jardek and Babka had not been born in Turkey, they had come there as refugees from Poland during the last world war. In those days Jardek had worked in the underground helping people to escape from Poland. In the end someone had betrayed him and he and Babka had to escape themselves. They had very little money, for by profession Jardek was a teacher of dancing and during the war there had not been many who wanted to learn to dance. So when they found the little tumbledown whitewashed cottage in the Turkish village, which cost almost nothing, they were grateful and settled down. At once Jardek, who was clever with his hands, set about repairing the cottage outside, while Babka put the inside in order. This took some time. Then, just as everything was tidy, Olga was born.

"Praise be to God," Jardek had said. "Now we have everything – a home and a child." He said this in Polish because at that time it was the only language that he spoke and in fact he never managed more than a few words of any other.

★ ★ ★

The year this story begins was the year that Francesco was ten, Gussie was nine and Anna was eight. The summer was a very special summer for they were staying two whole months with Jardek and Babka. This was because in the autumn Christopher was having an exhibition of his pictures at the other end of Turkey. Two months would give him time to get his pictures frames and a few more painted. More important, it would give Togo a real rest, which he would need if he was to pull the caravan to the other end of Turkey, for it was a journey of many, many miles and he was not young any more.

The two months in the village would also give time to discuss an important plan. Jardek, when the children stayed in his cottage had, as a matter of course, given them all dancing lessons. What was the use of having a highly skilled ballet teacher for a grandfather if you did not learn to dance? Jardek had no success with the boys; they danced better than most boys because they had been properly taught, but that special little spark for which Jardek searched was not there.

It was different, though, with Anna. From the time she could walk she had only to hear music and she had to dance. When she was little Jardek had just played tunes on his violin and let Anna dance to amuse herself. When she was six he had begun to give her lessons. Nothing strenuous – just the five positions and exercises and simple steps. But he had always known that here, in his own grandchild, was that rare special spark for which he had always searched.

Family discussions were noisy and there was much laughter because only Olga spoke everyone's language. Christopher refused to speak any language but English except when he was in France, when he would, if pushed, speak French, but with a strong English accent. This English accent was quite unnecessary for he could, as his children knew, speak perfect French. Olga had fairly correct English but spoke with a strong Polish accent. Christopher insisted that his children should speak English so, as Olga taught them their lessons, she spoke English most of the time. But Jardek and Babka spoke a mixture, mostly it was Polish but with English or Turkish words thrown in.

The discussion that summer was of course about Anna. It was no longer right, Jardek had decided, that Anna should only have dancing lessons when they stayed at the cottage. It was now time she began serious work. This year, when Christopher took his family to his exhibition, Anna must be left behind.

Anna could not think of her family going away without tears coming into her eyes. However, she knew of course that as she was to be a dancer – anything else was unthinkable – sacrifices must be made. Besides, though she loved her mother and father most, she also loved Jardek and Babka.

That Anna must have more dancing lessons was accepted by Christopher and Olga. Christopher, remembering his own stormy childhood when no one would allow him to learn to be an artist, would as soon as shot Togo as think of depriving Anna of her dancing lessons.

Because everything was more or less settled about Anna, that did not stop the endless discussions for as a family they all loved discussions and the more excited they got the better. But that summer morning when this story starts, although all the family were at breakfast, almost nothing was said. This was because it was so dreadfully hot. Never before had any of them known such stifling heat or such odd-looking weather. The sun was hidden behind a sulphur-coloured sky. Nobody felt like food but Olga insisted each child finished their yoghurt and ate one slice of bread with olives.

The children were to take one of Christopher's pictures to be framed. The frame maker lived in a village over the next hill about three miles away. There was no suggestion that they need not all go for they had always done everything together. Christopher looked up at the molten sky.

"I would take the caravan but I don't like spoiling poor old Togo's holiday by harnessing him up in this heat, and though the light is vile I must work today."

The children did not answer, they had all they could do forcing down their bread and olives.

"Perhaps," Olga suggested, "the children could the picture take tomorrow. Then today we will have school."

That settled it, nobody wanted the long walk in the sun, but they wanted lessons less. Anna felt this particularly for she knew Jardek was feeling too hot to give her a dancing lesson that day, but she hoped it might be cooler tomorrow. Christopher felt in his pocket and gave Francesco some money.

"Get some fruit and cold drinks and don't attempt to come back until the late afternoon."

The children got up and put on their hats. Then something – they did not know what – made them all turn just to look at Christopher, Olga, Jardek and Babka where they sat drinking their tea.

2. The Village That Went Away

MY GOODNESS, IT was hot walking to the next village! Used as the children were to heat they streamed with perspiration until they were wet all over. To make them hotter there was just a dirt track to the other village, so the dust was terrible. As they walked in single file, Francesco leading and carrying the canvas, Gussie next and Anna last, Anna particularly became brown with the dust that stuck to her.

When they got to the village it almost seemed like a wasted walk for the picture framer was asleep on his bed. He did open one eye but he refused to take an interest in any picture. So Francesco leant the canvas against the wall, feeling certain the picture framer would remember it when he woke up, for he was very fond of earning money and a great admirer of Christopher's paintings.

The children bought some figs, a vine leaf of mulberries

for each of them, and a bottle apiece of lemonade. Then they looked for a place in the shade where they could have a picnic.

"It's rather a long way," said Francesco, "but I think we climb up the hill as far as those cactuses, they're the best shade there is. It's much too hot to stay in this village."

Gussie groaned.

"If I don't lie down soon I'll drop down."

But Anna sided with Francesco.

"He's right, Gussie, that cactus hedge is quite thick, it's real proper shade."

When the children reached the cactus trees they were so hot and tired that they just flopped down in the shade panting, unable even to take a drink of lemonade. Then after a long time, Francesco said in a puzzled voice:

"Have you noticed something? How is it there aren't any birds?"

Gussie stared round.

"I expect they've gone somewhere cooler, and I don't blame them."

"This is the third day they've been gone," Anna told them. "Two days ago before my dancing lesson I am putting on my shoes and on our hill there were thousands of birds. Then they all flew away and they haven't come back."

Gussie reached out for his bottle of lemonade and his vine leaf of mulberries. It was then he noticed a horse in the next field.

"Look, I think that horse has gone mad."

Francesco and Anna looked where Gussie was pointing. The horse was old and thin but it was behaving as if it was a foal, rushing round bucking. The children stared at the horse in amazement.

"You can go mad when it's hot," Gussie stated. "Sometimes I am reading that dogs can."

"You can't get hydrophobia just because it's hot," Francesco told him, "but perhaps if it's very hot like today it can make you a bit strange."

Anna suddenly burst out in a voice which sounded as if she easily might cry.

"I don't like it; everything feels strange. I didn't like the birds going away, now the sky looks odd and now that horse."

Francesco thought Anna was being silly.

"Drink some lemonade, it's just that you're thirsty and it's so hot."

It was as Francesco said this that it began to happen. There was a roaring sound as if a very fast train was coming out of a tunnel pushing blazing hot air in front of it. Then the earth behaved as if it was the sea. It rocked to and fro like waves, and as it rocked the children were rolled and tossed around. Over and over they went. Then, after what seemed like ages, just as suddenly as it had started to move, the earth stood still again.

For a long time the children lay just where the earth had thrown them. Then one after another they sat up and at once noticed two extraordinary things. First the hillside, which had been smooth except for the dirt path, was now cut up as if a giant had stamped and had cracked it open. The other thing they noticed was that now, instead of being hot, it was turning cold, much colder than the children, who had always lived in hot countries, had known it could be.

It seemed as if the strange terrible thing that had happened had taken from the children the power of speech. Gussie did ask:

"What happened?"

And Francesco did answer:

"I don't know."

Then, without any more talking, as best they could because of the cracks in the earth, the children hurried up the hill towards home. At the top of the hill they stopped. Opposite them they should have seen the village quite distinctly. Jardek and Babka's little cottage with Togo in the field opposite which he shared with some cows and a donkey. The other cottages, the shops, the tea house, and the little mosque. But none of it was there. Where the village had been there was nothing – nothing at all.

3. Sir William

SIR WILLIAM HOOGLE was a famous archaeologist and writer. He was travelling in Turkey when the earthquake happened which destroyed Jardek and Babka's village, in fact he was near enough to feel the earth tremors himself. On the radio he heard how terrible an earthquake it had been for those living at the centre of the disaster. He learnt about the village which had disappeared, and of how difficult it was to carry out rescue work because the ground was so full of fissures that no aeroplane could land. Such help as was reaching the afflicted areas was being dropped by parachute.

Now Sir William not only spoke Turkish but also understood most of the local dialects. In his mind he could see the planes flying over the scene of the earthquake, dropping bundles by parachute on people almost certainly too shocked by what had happened to know how to use what they were being given. There were of course doctors and nurses being dropped but would they have time to help anybody but the injured?

"I think I could be of use," Sir William told himself. "Anyhow, I shall go and find out."

All round the areas affected by the earthquake, railway lines had become twisted, the roads had fissures across them and were blocked by piles of rubble which had once been buildings. If there is one kind of help no country wants in times of national disaster it is unskilled labour. So when Sir William asked officials how he could be transported to the scene of the earthquake he was told politely – for he was very distinguished – but firmly he could not go. As soon as aeroplanes could land help was coming, meanwhile those on the spot were doing all that could be done.

Sir William quite understood the officials. After all, he was not a specialist in disaster work, but all the same he was still convinced he could be of use. So he bought a camel – he turned out to be very bad-tempered – called Muzzaffer, filled a light case with his toilet articles and a change of clothes and things he thought might be useful and rode off in the direction of the afflicted part of the country.

It was a long way for Sir William to ride for he had to make constant detours to avoid fissures. His journey was not helped by Muzzaffer, who complained loudly the whole way that Sir William and the case were too heavy for him – which was not true – and that he hated earthquakes. All the same he carried Sir William safely first to the village where the children had taken Christopher's picture to be framed, and then to the centre of the disaster area. From the moment they saw their village had gone a sort of silent frenzy had come over the children, then, without saying a word, they stumbled and ran all the way to where they thought the little house had been. There they knelt down and dug and dug with their fingers. But though they dug without stopping they could not find any sign of their family – just nothing – nothing at all.

Nor was the place where their own little house had been the only place where the children dug, they dug in the field Togo had shared with the cows and the donkey. They dug where they thought the tea house had been. They dug where the shop had once stood. They dug for the other cottages and the mosque. On they went, dig, dig, dig until their nails were broken and their hands covered in blood. And still they never spoke.

Although the children's own village was gone others were not, but the damage everywhere was terrible and very widespread so each district had to help itself. To begin with all who were not injured tried to get the wounded out from under fallen buildings. Presently the first of the aeroplanes arrived and a doctor, a nurse and a tent came down by parachute. Later came more doctors and nurses and piles of blankets and packets of food. It was when the blankets arrived that the people noticed how cold it was. By now the tent was up and all the wounded that could be found had been taken into it. The doctors then decided that as it would soon be dark looking for wounded must stop for that day, that the women should build a fire and cook a meal, but that everyone else should put a blanket round them and search the countryside for any people who might be homeless and bring them to the tent.

It was only by accident that the children were found, for who would look for people in a village which had disappeared? But a man and a boy decided to climb the hill to see if anyone was about on the other side. That was how they fell over the children. At no time did the children speak much Turkish and now they couldn't speak at all, they couldn't even hear, they just went on dig, dig, dig. The man, who had a big voice, roared for help and presently two more men turned up and after discussion the three men took off their blankets, rolled the children in them, picked them up, slung them over their shoulders and, sending the boy ahead to tell the doctors what they had found, they marched off towards the tent.

The children knew nothing of what happened after that, for the doctor who examined them almost at once gave them an injection and laid them in the hospital part of the tent covered in blankets.

The arrival of Sir William two days later on Muzzaffer caused quite a sensation in what was now called "Camp A". By that time help of every kind had arrived: troops to mend and clear the roads, helicopters to fly wounded to the hospitals, rescue squads to dig in the ruins and help of other types, particularly clothes, food and medicines. A very important man who knew the neighbourhood was in charge of relief work so it was to him Sir William, with a parcel under his arm, presented himself. He explained who he was and asked if there was any way in which he could be of service.

"You are British?" asked the official.

Sir William nodded.

"I am."

"Then you may be able to help me. We have in camp three children. We believe them to be British."

Sir William liked the facts.

"Why?"

The official opened a drawer and took out a large envelope. "The children do not know this. But caught in a crater we found the remains of what probably was a caravan, there was little left of it but this." He took out of the envelope a British passport. "This belonged, as you can see, to a man called Christopher Docksay. His wife's name was Olga and there are three children listed – Francesco, Augustus and Anna."

"Did Christopher Docksay live here?" Sir William asked.

"No, not live," the official explained. "But the locals say that Madame Docksay was the daughter of an old Pole who, with his wife, lived in that village which has gone. This daughter, whose name was Olga, married this Christopher Docksay and every year they came to stay, travelling by caravan. He was an artist."

"He was indeed," Sir William agreed. "He'll be a great loss. You say the locals told you all about the family but what do the children say?"

The official threw up his hands.

"The doctors say it is shock and will pass, but so far the children have said nothing, not to each other, not to us. They just sit, well-behaved you understand, but like deaf mutes. They were found digging with their fingers for their family where that village once stood. The doctors say the children do not yet want to remember, when they do they will talk."

Sir William thought for a moment, then he showed the official the parcel under his arm.

"I found this today. It is a picture of Christopher Docksay's, the children took it to the village over that hill to be framed on the day of the earthquake. The picture framer was showing it to everybody because the painting is of the village which has gone. I paid him for his work and promised to see that the picture was delivered to Christopher Docksay's executors, whoever they may be. If the doctors permit I shall show this picture to the children. It might get through to them."

The children could not stop shivering. They sat on the floor of the tent with blankets round them. One of the nurses had combed their hair and washed their faces and they had been fed with soup. They paid no attention when a doctor led Sir William over to them. Nor were they interested when Sir William sat down opposite to them and opened a flat parcel. Then he spun the contents of the parcel round so that it faced them.

There was the little house just as they had last seen it except that on the porch only Olga, Jardek and Babka were drinking tea for, of course, Christopher was painting the picture. There was a second's pause, then Francesco fainted, Gussie was sick and Anna screamed.

Mr Cecil Docksay
'Dunroamin'
The Crescent
Fyton Essex
ENGLAND.

4. The Uncle

Cecil Docksay lived with his wife Mabel in Essex. His house was in a place called Fyton. Much of Essex is very pretty but Fyton was not because it was mostly badly designed new houses which crowded round the church, a village green and three thatched cottages. But Cecil Docksay thought his house perfect because, as he was always saying, it was so labour-saving and therefore easy to run.

It was a neat house outside and in. Upstairs it had three bedrooms: one the big main room which they shared, two small spare rooms in which everything was always in dust-sheets because they never had a visitor to stay. There was, too, a magnificent bathroom.

Downstairs there was a big room which they called the lounge. This was full of green velvet furniture and had a white wallpaper with a design on it of trellis work up which

climbed ivy. On the walls there were no pictures but a trail of
ceramic geese in full flight.

The lounge looked on to the garden, which was even
more labour-saving than the house for everything in it was
made of plastic. The garden was covered in concrete
pretending to be crazy paving. In the middle of the concrete
there was a small pool by which sat two scarlet gnomes
apparently fishing, only there were no fish in the pool, not
even a tadpole in the spring. Instead of flower beds there were
metal containers and in these lived plastic plants which were
changed to suit the season. In the spring they were full of
daffodils and hyacinths. Then those were sponged and put
away and out came rose trees and other summer flowers.
When the autumn came it was goodbye to the summer
flowers and a splendid show of plastic chrysanthemums took
their place. Everybody else living in Fyton grew real flowers
and, though their gardens were small, they worked very hard
to make them look and smell beautiful.

"So foolish," Cecil Docksay would say to Mabel as he
watched their neighbours struggling with greenfly or dead-
heading their real chrysanthemums. "What I say is why make
work?"

Mabel did not answer for she liked real flowers but to say
so would only mean an argument.

At the front of the house was the dining room, in which
the table and chairs were made of something which looked
like wood but was unmarkable, because it was heat-resisting,
dirt-resisting – in fact there was nothing it did not resist

including being nice to look at.

The kitchen was Mabel's pride. It was quite a large room and had been bought exactly as it stood at an exhibition called "The Home Beautiful". It was the most labour-saving kitchen ever invented. The house was called Dunroamin.

The day the letter arrived was wet and stormy. Cecil and Mabel Docksay were having breakfast, Cecil looking with pride at the way their plastic rose tree stood stiff and resistant to the rain and wind, while their neighbours' roses, which had been beautiful, took on that sad stuck-together look which roses have on wet days.

Mabel Docksay had always been a shy person. Her mother had been good-looking and popular with a large circle of friends. She would have liked to have a pretty little girl of whom she could have been proud. So it was annoying for her that she had a child who tried to make herself smaller than she was so that she would not be noticed. If her father had been about he would have understood and sympathized with Mabel for he was shy himself, but he was out at work all day so had never seem much of his daughter.

Mabel had worked hard at school but she was more a plodder than clever, so she was not able to fulfil her dream which was to be sent to a university, which would mean living away from home. Instead she had settled for a job in the local bank. "Well, I suppose at least it's a safe job," her mother had said to her friends, "and she needs a safe job, poor darling, for she's so shy and I'm afraid rather dull, so she will never marry." Of course Mabel knew this was what her mother believed so she thought herself the luckiest girl in the world when the assistant manager at the bank, Cecil Docksay, asked her to marry him. She was so grateful to be asked, which meant getting away from home and living in a house of her own, that she mistook gratitude for love. Her father did worry about the marriage for he thought Cecil Docksay a terribly dull man.

"You're very young, Mabel," he had said. "Don't rush into anything you might regret."

Mabel with shining eyes had replied:

"I'm rushing to do what I want to do."

Just about the time Cecil Docksay, by then manager, retired from the bank his father and mother died so, since Christopher was forgotten, he inherited all the money there was and was able to buy Dunroamin. Mabel thought Dunroamin was a pleasant house and knew she should be happy to live in it and grateful to dear Cecil for buying it, but somehow she didn't feel any of these things – only rather depressed.

Who wants two silly gnomes? she thought resentfully and secretly looked enviously out of her windows at other people's children. Oh, if only she and Cecil had had a child!

On the wet and stormy morning when the postman knocked on the door Mabel jumped up to get the post, for Cecil was not the sort of man whom anyone would ask to open a front door.

There was only the one letter – a long white envelope with Turkish stamps. Cecil opened the envelope carefully with a knife for it was a good envelope which could be used again, and he was nothing if not careful. He noticed it had been sent from a hotel in Istanbul. Then he looked at the end of the letter to see who had signed it but he couldn't read the signature. But the hotel secretary who had typed the letter had typed at the bottom "Sir William Hoogle". Cecil knew that name for having been a bank manager he prided himself on knowing who was who.

All the papers had carried the news that Christopher Docksay had been killed in the earthquake. To Cecil, Christopher's name was not one to be mentioned, for having run away to Paris with his father's possessions he was a thief so best forgotten. In Fyton it had not yet crossed anyone's mind that the odd Mr and Mrs Docksay who lived in Dunroamin and planted plastic flowers instead of real ones could possibly be related to anyone famous, especially not to a famous artist.

On the radio the newscaster had said that of recent years Christopher's pictures had fetched a lot of money, which had made Mabel ask:

"Are you his heir, dear?"

"I suppose so," Cecil had agreed. "No doubt someone will communicate in time." Now, as he started to read his letter, he said to Mabel: "This is from Turkey, no doubt about Christopher's estate. Wonderful how quick they were finding my address."

But as Cecil read the letter a great change came over him. He made so many grunts and growls that Mabel trembled.

That was how she saw his colour change from yellow (he was a pasty man) to red and finally to purple. When he came to the last word he thumped his fist on the table so hard that if anything could have marked it that would have.

"I won't have it! Prying busybody! Why should he take it upon himself to find my address? How does he dare dictate to me what I should do or not do?"

"Who, dear?" Mabel asked.

Cecil could hardly speak he was so angry.

"Sir William Hoogle. It seems Christopher was married to some Polish woman and they had three children."

Mabel did not know who Sir William Hoogle was, or what Cecil was so angry about, so she said, trying not to sound as thrilled as she felt:

"Three children!"

Cecil could have hit Mabel for repeating every word he said. He'd give her something to repeat.

"Listen!" he roared. "This is the last paragraph of the letter: 'I plan to deliver the children to you at the end of the week. I will cable the time of our arrival.' "

The day after Sir William arrived at Camp A the children were better. The terrible cold which followed the earthquake was gone, so they sat in the sun outside the hospital tent to eat their breakfast and that's where Sir William found them. They looked, he thought, a pathetic lot of little ragamuffins, for you can't be thrown about by an earthquake and finish up either clean or tidy.

"You lot want some new clothes," he said. "We must go shopping."

Anna looked surprised at such ignorance.

"There are not shops here and the clothes at the relief places are not yet for children."

"Some will be coming," Gussie explained. "The nurse told us."

"I don't think we'll wait for that," said Sir William. "Let's go to Istanbul. Good shops there."

The children stared at him. Of course they had heard of Istanbul but they had never been there. Christopher had never gone to a town unless he had to. Towns were tiresome about parking a caravan. Francesco, used to travelling at a speed chosen by Togo, suggested:

"Isn't Istanbul rather a long way away?"

Sir William took a cigar from his pocket and lit it.

"A long way away from where?" he asked.

Well, that was a question. It brought all three children slap up against the things they did not want to think about. Where now was home? Everybody was gone – Christopher, Olga, Jardek, Babka and Togo, the little house and the caravan. When they went away from where they were now they had no place at all to come back to.

Francesco gave a shiver as if it was cold again. Gussie looked as if he might be going to be sick, which he had been off and on since the earthquake, and two tears trickled down Anna's cheeks.

"I'm sorry," she choked, "but you shouldn't have asked

that."

"Nonsense!" retorted Sir William. "You can't live in a hospital tent for ever. You have been given into my charge for the time being and I don't intend to let you out of my sight until I see you settled. Now, Francesco, you are the eldest. Tell me what you know of your family."

Francesco wanted to be helpful but all the family he knew were dead. However, Sir William was aware of that so he must mean father away relations.

Then Gussie said:

"There was the father of our father." He turned to Francesco and Anna. "He was that horrible man who would not let Christopher paint."

Francesco remembered, for Christopher had often told the story. He looked at Sir William.

"So our father had to take things from the house to sell for the air fare to Paris where he must learn to paint."

Sir William nodded.

"Good thing he did, for he became a very fine painter. Do you know where this grandfather of yours lived?"

All the children shook their heads. Never once had they heard a place mentioned and, never having been to England, they would not have remembered if they had. Then another piece of information came into Gussie's memory.

"The brother of our father was already in a bank while Christopher is in a school." He looked triumphantly at Francesco and Anna. "You remember Christopher telling us that?"

They did indeed. Riding along a yellow dusty road in Pakistan. It was not said to them but to Olga.

"This is the life, Olga. I love it. The sun to beat on your head, the smell of spices up your nose and a caravan for a home. And to think if my father had had his way I'd be shut up in a bank. I might even be on the road to becoming a bank manager. I suppose Cecil is one by now unless he's retired."

Recalling that scene hurt so much the children would have wished to change the subject, but they liked Sir William and he was trying to help so Francesco said to the others:

"I suppose Cecil is a bank manager now."

Sir William was not the sort of man who missed anything anybody said.

"Who is Cecil?"

Christopher had told so many funny stories about his brother Cecil it seemed strange anybody didn't know who he was.

"He is the brother of our father. He is The Uncle," Gussie explained. "He is already in a bank when Christopher is at school."

"Is he married?" Sir William asked.

The children shook their heads.

"We do not know, he was in a bank when our father is first leaving to paint in Paris," Francesco explained. "For two years our father sends his father and mother a Christmas card."

"With funny drawings of himself on them," Gussie added.

"And his address," Anna reminded them.

"But the father is still angry," said Francesco. "He never

answered. Never at all."

Sir William saw he had got all there was to know out of the children. He had plenty of influence and Docksay was an uncommon name. If any of the family were alive he would run them to earth.

"The army say the runway will be open tomorrow, in which case we should get a plane for Istanbul. From there I will telephone London to inquire after your relations."

"But they don't sound very nice," said Gussie.

Sir William smiled comfortingly.

"If we find them you can try them out. I shan't be far away, I'll keep in touch."

Francesco remembered that Sir William did not know the important thing.

"Anna has to learn to dance."

"Real proper learning," Gussie added. "For Jardek, our mother's father, was a great teacher and he said Anna was special, she was going to be such a dancer as he had always prayed he would teach."

Sir William knew very little about dancing, but he was an optimist and did not believe in imagining difficulties – time enough to worry when they cropped up.

"I feel sure dancing classes can be arranged," he said calmly. "But the first thing is to find out if you have relations and where."

Sir William did his best to give the children a splendid time in Istanbul. He also bought them new clothes, such as they had never owned: grey flannel shorts for the boys with shirts and ties, and two good cotton frocks for Anna. Also there were pullovers for them all in case it turned cold. Then, on the fourth day, Sir William had a telephone call from London. He told the children the news at once.

"You have got relations. Your grandparents are dead but your Uncle Cecil is alive and you have an Aunt Mabel. They live in a house called Dunroamin in a place called Fyton. I am writing to them today to explain the situation and to say I will deliver you to them at the end of the week."

5. The Decision

IT WAS A stormy morning inside as well as out in Dunroamin after the letter arrived. Angry words flew round the dining room like hailstones.

"We'll go away, Mabel. We'll lock up the house."

"We couldn't do that for long, dear," said Mabel. "I mean, it's our home, where should we go?"

"I'll send a cable to Istanbul to say you are ill, something infectious so we are unable even to see the children."

"But," squeaked Mabel, who had almost lost her voice trying to be heard over Cecil's shouts, "everybody knows I'm not ill. They see me shopping every day."

"I'll see my solicitor, I'm sure nobody can be forced to take in their brother's children, especially a brother who is a thief."

Mabel thought of something he would care about.

"Wouldn't it look very bad if it came out that we'd refused to have them?"

"How can it come out? The children are in Turkey. I suppose there are orphanages in Turkey."

"Not for British children, dear."

Cecil looked back at his letter.

"They are only half British, their mother was a Pole. Why don't their Polish relations have them?"

"Perhaps there aren't any," said Mabel. "Anyway, I don't see how you can suggest that. I mean, wouldn't this Sir William think it was odd?"

In the end, though very grudgingly, Cecil accepted that for the time being he was beaten. He simply could not cable Sir William to say, "No. I won't have the children."

"We must just hope there is some money," he said. "Then we can pack the lot off to boarding schools; the papers have been saying his pictures sold well."

"Yes, dear, they did," said Mabel, thankful to be able to agree about one thing at least, though secretly not accepting the boarding schools.

Then Cecil thought of something new to be cross about.

"If only we had bought a smaller house with no spare bedrooms, we couldn't have had the children. That was your fault, Mabel, you would have that kitchen."

Mabel was used to being blamed for things she had not done, so it was no surprise to her to hear it was her fault Cecil had bought Dunroamin. Though actually the first she had known of the purchase was when Cecil had said:

"I have bought a house."

So she changed the subject.

"What shall we do if this Sir William wants to stay the night?"

"We can't have him, thank goodness. In his letter he says there are two boys and a girl. That uses up the two rooms; in any case I have no intention of this Sir William or any other busybody crossing the threshold. If I have to bring up my brother's children I shall do it in my own way. I shall fly to Istanbul and collect the children. Imagine Sir William writing 'I will cable time of arrival'! Who does he think he is? Any cabling time of arrival will be done by me."

While all this arguing was going on in Dunroamin the children were getting to know Sir William, whom they called S'William, for they had never known a "Sir" and never seen the name written, and the more they got to know him the more they liked him. He was so sensible and unfussy. Without being told he knew they could not eat proper food since the earthquake, so he let them have what they liked. If all Anna wanted was hard boiled eggs and olives in a sandwich that was all she liked so why argue? If Gussie mostly fancied fruit and fizzy lemonade then let him live on them. Black coffee with perhaps an ice cream was not Sir William's idea of a nourishing meal but if it was Francesco's that was his business. He only made one food rule.

"I don't mind what you kids eat, but it's not much, so see there's always some of what you like to hand. After all, what's to prevent you being hungry in the middle of the night? And, believe me, if all else fails two or three buns at midnight are a splendidly filling meal."

After one midnight meal of figs, buns and bars of chocolate Gussie said to Francesco:

"I think things to eat in bed is a good idea, in fact only eating when you want to is a good idea. I plan to go on doing that when we get to The Uncle."

"An uncle, especially a British uncle, eats food at proper times, S'William told me," replied Francesco.

"I expect we can make him see our way is simpler," Gussie said. "After all, he ought to be glad, for it saves cooking and laying tables and all that."

Francesco was getting sleepy – buns at night do have that effect.

"S'William said he expected living with The Uncle would turn out all right, that things often do. So perhaps he'll understand about food."

Sir William, who was seldom surprised by anything, was amazed when the cable arrived. For a man who lived in a house called Dunroamin did not sound as if, without a word of warning, he would roam as far as Istanbul. He was also annoyed for he did not want an unknown companion landed on him for the flight home, so he bought four tickets in an aeroplane going to London and wired the flight number and time of arrival to Uncle Cecil. Then he called the children.

"Go and pack, kids. We leave for London in two hours."

He gave an envelope to Francesco. "I don't expect you'll ever need this but if you do, write to me at this address. No doubt your Uncle Cecil is a splendid fellow but sometimes an outsider can help. Don't worry if, having written to me, it's weeks before you get an answer for I am always travelling, in fact I'm only going to stay one night in London then I'm off to Alaska. And, by the way, I'm holding on to your father's picture for you. Some more may turn up but in the meantime it seems to be all you possess, so I should keep it a secret if I were you. Proper wolves there are in the picture business."

It's impossible for anything to happen slowly at an airport. The children had only just got their breath back from the excitement of the journey when they found themselves staring at a strange man who was almost like Christopher only somehow quite the opposite.

The man said:

"I am your Uncle Cecil. Wait over there while I talk to Sir William."

Over there, which was by an advice counter, Anna whispered to the boys:

"I wish he didn't look like Christopher because I don't think I'm going to like him."

"He speaks," Gussie said, "like a very old dry biscuit."

Sir William during the flight had told Francesco a lot of things including the fact that they might not take to their uncle right away – nor he to them – there would have to be give and take on both sides. So now Francesco tried to explain this to the others.

"S'William said we mightn't like The Uncle at first but we must give time."

"I don't need time," Gussie retorted. "I hate him now this very minute."

Sir William was thinking that very same thing. He simply loathed leaving the children with their uncle but what could he do? This Uncle Cecil was their legal guardian. In any case in his travelling life there was no place for three children. So he did the best he could. He cut the goodbyes short.

"Goodbye, kids," he called out. "Let's hear from you some time." Then he waved, turned and was swallowed up in the crowd.

6. The Aunt

THE BOYS, WHO shared the larger of the two bedrooms, woke up early the next morning.

Gussie sat up and looked round.

"What a horrible room!"

Francesco sat up too.

"I think it's just so clean and we aren't used to rooms that are as clean as this."

"The hotel room in Istanbul was very clean," Gussie argued, "but it didn't look like this."

Francesco saw suddenly something that was wrong with the room.

"There aren't any pictures, even the hotel in Istanbul had pictures, not very nice but they had them. As a matter of fact there aren't any in the whole house."

"I wish," said Gussie, "we'd kept our picture, it would be

something of us, now there is nothing."

"S'William was right, though, if it was here it would be sold."

"What, by wolves like he said?"

Francesco lowered his voice to a whisper.

"No. By The Uncle. I do not think he is pleased we have no money."

Gussie tried to remember last night but it was a blur.

"I remember The Uncle driving us in his motorcar, it was a long way and I went to sleep."

"When we got to this house The Aunt was in the hall and she said supper was ready and we should wash," Francesco prompted him.

"And did we?" Gussie asked.

"Yes, and then we went into a room for eating and there was a dish rolled up in thick grey stuff like a blanket. The Aunt said it was steak and kidney pudding. You looked at it and at once you were sick so you went to bed."

"Fancy, and I do not remember," said Gussie. "But then I've been sick a lot lately."

Francesco went on.

"Anna began to cry, just a little at first but then louder and louder so she went to bed. The Aunt took her."

"And you?" Gussie asked. "You stayed?"

"Yes, not to eat, that I could not, but The Aunt gave me a glass of milk with chocolate in it. The Uncle said she should not give in, children should eat what they were given, but she said it wouldn't hurt for once, it had been a tiring day."

"What else did The Uncle say?"

Francesco clasped his hands round his knees.

"He said we spoke English very bad, you remember Christopher said that too. That now it is the summer holiday but soon we all go to school."

"Where?"

"There is a school in this place."

"For Anna too?"

Francesco nodded.

"That is the bad thing. I told him Anna could not go to an ordinary school, she must go where there is good training to dance, but he made a sort of spitting sound and then he said: 'I don't hold with dancing nor ever will.'"

Gussie was shocked.

"Did you explain what Jardek had said?"

"Every single word and on each word he made more spitting noises. It is no good hoping, Gussie. The Uncle will not pay for Anna to learn to dance."

Gussie was so shocked he did not answer for quite a while. Then he got out of bed and began putting on his clothes.

"Quick, we must hurry."

Francesco watched him.

"Hurry where?"

"To S'William, of course, to sell our picture to pay for Anna to learn. We must get it before he goes to Alaska."

Francesco shook his head.

"Do you think I did not think of that? S'William is in

London, we are a long way from there, we should have to take a train, and we have no money, no money at all."

Often when there was to be a picture exhibition Christopher had driven the caravan to a place where there was a telephone. Gussie remembered this.

"Then we must telephone."

Francesco felt under his pillow and brought out Sir William's envelope. He passed it to Gussie.

"I thought of that but look, there is only an address."

Gussie took out the piece of paper inside the envelope and saw this was true. There was just an address scrawled across it but no telephone number. He put the paper back in the envelope and gave it to Francesco.

"Then what shall we do?"

"First take off your clothes and get back into bed. In this house all is arranged. I think we will bath before we dress. The Aunt said so. Then we must learn this address by heart in case we lose the envelope."

"Can't we hide it somewhere?"

Francesco looked round the room.

"Where?"

Gussie had undressed again. Now he put on his pyjamas.

"Let's look."

At that moment they heard someone coming up the stairs so, quick as a grasshopper, Gussie got back into bed while Francesco shoved the envelope under his pillow.

Aunt Mabel opened the door. None of them had taken Aunt Mabel in last night for Gussie and Anna were both too wretched and too tired to notice anybody, and Francesco was talking to his uncle. But now the boys had a chance to study her and very odd they thought she was. "Like a mouse," Gussie described her later, "afraid to move in case a cat is coming."

The oddest thing about Aunt Mabel was her voice. It was as if she had to push at her words to make them sound at all, and if she said much she seemed to run out of breath.

To look at, too, she was to the children surprising. Dressed in a shapeless flowered dress and an apron which seemed to hold her together. She had hair which, though no doubt she had put pins in it, seemed to be falling down. As a result the general effect was crumpled. This amazed the boys for the only British woman they had looked at was the Queen, whose picture Olga stuck up with a pin during lessons. The picture was of the Queen at the Flower Show and was much admired by the three children, who had supposed that was how all British ladies looked.

"Good morning, dears," Aunt Mabel puffed. "Time for baths. You can go now, Francesco, for your uncle has finished with the bathroom. You will have to run along as you are as you have no dressing-gowns."

In the caravan or when staying with Jardek and Babka, there had been no use for dressing-gowns, though Christopher had an old one he occasionally put on. Bathing had happened when it could. Sometimes water was heated and poured into a tub and was used by all the family in turn. More often they bathed where everybody else did, in a wayside stream, a lake or perhaps a river. For ordinary washing there was always cold water and a tin basin.

Francesco wondered if The Aunt was blaming S'William for not buying them dressing-gowns.

"In the hotel in Istanbul we had no use for dressing-gowns for in each bedroom was a bath which was ours alone."

The glory of that memory rang in Francesco's voice.

Aunt Mabel was obviously impressed, in fact she seemed unable to answer for her mouth just opened and shut like a fish's.

"S'William bought us all the beautiful clothes we have," said Gussie.

Aunt Mabel's voice sounded more faint and jerky than ever.

"Oh dear, I hope your uncle does not know that for he would feel he ought to pay him."

Gussie was shocked.

"A present is a present, it is rude to wish to pay."

Aunt Mabel, as if her legs would no longer hold her upright, sank on to the end of Francesco's bed. She spoke in a whisper:

"In time you will understand your uncle" – she did not sound as if that was a promise. "But until you do, dears, will you try not to annoy him?"

"What is it that annoys him?" Gussie asked.

Aunt Mabel squeezed her hands together.

"Please, please, dears, don't ask him to let Anna dance. You see, to him dancing is not right."

The boys gaped at her. Naturally, with a grandfather like Jardek, dancing was like painting or any art – a gift from God to be treasured and worked at. Had not Olga explained this to them almost every day? Gussie supposed The Aunt did not understand.

"Jardek – he was the father of our mother – was a great teacher of ballet in Warsaw. When he had to leave and come to Turkey he taught us. Francesco and me we have no gift but Anna has."

Francesco added:

"Always Jardek knew this. 'She has the real special spark,' he said: 'always I have searched and now I am rewarded to find it in my own granddaughter.'"

"Not to let her learn," said Gussie firmly, "is a sin – a bad sin."

The voice of Uncle Cecil roared up the stairs.

"What's going on, Mabel? Those children should be bathed and dressed by now."

Aunt Mabel scuttled to the door.

"Hurry, boys," she gasped. "Hurry."

Francesco and Gussie looked at each other then Francesco gave Gussie Sir William's envelope.

"Hide it somewhere while I have my bath. Afterwards we will talk for it is us who must arrange that Anna learns to dance."

7. *Money*

WHEN THE CHILDREN sat down to breakfast Uncle Cecil said:

"I make it a rule at meals that nothing is said unless it is important or uplifting."

This was so off-putting that the children could only look at each other out of the corners of their eyes to say what they thought. When they had lived in the caravan or stayed with Jardek and Babka everyone had so much to say that all talked at once and seldom minded if no one was listening. Of course sometimes Christopher would bang on the table and shout "I will have hush" or something like that. Mostly this happened when a picture was going wrong, then the last way to describe what Christopher said was either important or uplifting.

By good luck the food was what the children liked and could eat – a cereal followed by boiled eggs – and though

Anna left half her egg in its shell Uncle Cecil did not notice so there was no trouble.

After breakfast the children were told by Uncle Cecil to go to their rooms to give their aunt a hand with the tidying up.

"Old beast!" Gussie muttered as they climbed the stairs. "He ought to have seen the way we helped Babka. I think he thinks we can't even make a bed."

Anna said to Francesco:

"If I bring a piece of ribbon will you plait my hair?"

Francesco was surprised.

"Why plait it, you never do?"

"It'll look awful plaited," said Gussie.

Anna darted into her bedroom and came out with a piece of red ribbon to match the red check cotton frock she was wearing which Sir William had bought for her. Anna had dark hair and big dark eyes, so even when she was too pale, which she was at the moment, red suited her.

"I wore my hair loose in Istanbul because I couldn't do it on top of my head" – she didn't need to say "as Olga did it" because the boys knew – "but I think this is a plait sort of house. I mean a plait is neat and this is a very neat place."

Francesco plaited her hair and tied the red bow on the end of the plait. It was a sad sort of thing to do for it reminded him of Togo who, on birthdays and at Christmas, had always had his tail plaited. But of course he did not tell the others what he was thinking. Instead he said to Anna:

"I'm glad you came in. Gussie and I have much to tell

you. The Uncle will not let you learn to dance, he thinks it is wrong."

Anna swung round to face Francesco. Her face was whiter than ever, especially round the mouth.

"I do not care what The Uncle thinks. I do not like him and I will dance. I must dance, you know what Jardek said."

Francesco remembered what he had told Gussie to do.

"Where did you put the envelope with S'William's address?"

That calmed Anna down.

"Good. I had forgotten we had his address. We will go now and tell him. He will understand and arrange everything."

Gussie showed Francesco the built-in cupboard.

"In such a house even a bottom shelf which is not used is covered with paper." He opened the cupboard door so the others could see. Each shelf was covered with a pale green washable lining paper with a pattern of leaves on it. "Under there at the back," he pointed to the bottom shelf, "is S'William's envelope. The Aunt will never look there."

"Good," said Francesco. Then he turned back to Anna. "This place is far from London where S'William is, and today he goes to Alaska. If he was in London, even if I had to walk, I would have gone to him and asked him to sell our picture."

Anna was not her father's daughter for nothing. There was desperation in her voice.

"I must learn," she said, "and from the best teacher. If we cannot sell the picture we must sell things from this house."

Francesco suddenly felt very much the eldest.

"No," he said firmly. "That we will never do. Olga taught to steal is wrong, you remember."

"I do," Gussie agreed. "That catechism we had to learn. It said 'Thou shalt not steal' and Olga said it was not truly stealing that Christopher did because it was from his own father."

"This would be from our own uncle," Anna argued.

"No," said Francesco. "You shall learn to dance but no one will steal."

Gussie thumped his chest.

"Francesco and me – we will earn the money. How do you think boys earn money in Britain?"

A procession of ways of earning money passed through the children's minds. Loading donkeys with wood, leading a camel from one place to another, calling conveyances for people, running errands; there were, especially in towns, a hundred ways of earning small coins and small coins added up.

"First," said Francesco, "we have to find the best place for learning dancing."

"Who would know?" asked Gussie. "The Uncle doesn't and I shouldn't think The Aunt does. Would a priest?"

Francesco was doubtful.

"This I don't know, but we could try. But while we are trying, Anna, you must practise."

Anna nodded.

"I did in Istanbul holding on to the end of the bed. But I

can't do much. Exercises done wrong can do harm. Then I have no shoes and it is difficult to be right when you only wear socks."

No shoes! The boys had not thought of that. Anna had had soft pink shoes tied on with ribbons. Jardek ordered them from a shop in Italy. But of course they were gone with everything else.

"I think shoes should be the first thing we should buy," said Gussie. "Then we find out where Anna must go to learn."

Aunt Mabel took the children shopping that first morning to give them some idea of Fyton. To the children, who had never been out of the Near or Far East, it was confusing for everything was different. Fyton, which had been a village, was growing into what is called "a new town". As a result it was full of young married couples. It seemed to the children that everybody owned a fat pink and white baby in a pram. There were older children as well, all well dressed and rushing about with shopping bags. They were amazed at the supermarket.

"These British must be very honest," Anna whispered to Francesco. "Imagine everything out where anybody can steal!"

"I think also they are very rich," said Francesco. "We have seen no beggars – no beggars at all."

Aunt Mabel wanted to get home to cook the lunch but she had come to a conclusion about the children. If there was to be any peace in the house she must keep them out of

Cecil's way as much as possible. Fortunately, he was out a good deal serving on committees and organizing things, but he was at home that morning so the children must stay out. Mabel opened her purse and took two tenpenny pieces out of it. She had no idea how she was going to explain where the two tenpenny pieces had gone for Cecil went through the accounts daily, but she would think of something and for the moment peace was more important. She showed the children the turning to Dunroamin and the clock on the Town Hall.

"You must start home at twelve-thirty, dears, so that you have time to wash before lunch which is at one o'clock sharp. These," she gave the two tenpenny pieces to Francesco, "will buy you all ice creams."

When Aunt Mabel had pushed her way out of sight between perambulators the children examined the tenpenny pieces, which was the first English money they had seen. Anna clasped her hands together ecstatically.

"Perhaps The Aunt each day will give us such money for ices. Then soon I will have my shoes."

"It is a start," Francesco agreed, "but for dancing classes much money will be wanted."

Gussie again thumped his chest.

"Me, I have thought of a way."

"How?" asked Francesco and Anna.

"Up that road," Gussie pointed to the place he meant, "there is a little market, not like a big bazaar but things are sold from stalls."

"But we've nothing to sell," Francesco reminded him.

"Oh yes we have," said Gussie. "S'William gave two of everything for each. All we need is one, we can wear a blanket while the one is washed."

Anna saw the idea.

"And our suitcases. Our beautiful new suitcases! People must give money for those."

Francesco was carried away by the enthusiasm of the other two.

"No one, not even The Uncle, could mind that we sell what is ours. Now all we must do is find out how we can borrow a little stall."

8. Wally

THE CHILDREN WENT to have a look at the little market. They were connoisseurs of markets of every description; they thought very poorly of this one.

"No cooked food," Gussie grumbled. "There should always be cooked food in a market, it smells well so people come."

"But they do sell clothes," Francesco said, pointing to a stall which had clothes all round it on coat hangers.

They went up to the stall. Anna fingered a coat.

"But not good clothes like the one S'William gave us."

"What you kids want?" a voice asked. The children looked round and at first could not see who had spoken because he was behind the clothes. Then a boy about Francesco's age with bright red hair came round the stall. "This is me mum's stall but I'm lookin' arter it."

Gussie liked the look of the boy and, anyway, he expected everybody to be friends, at least he had until he met The Uncle.

"We aren't wanting to buy anything, we were wishing to know how you can have a little stall."

The boy stared at Gussie.

"You talk funny. Foreign, are you?"

"No," said Francesco, "we are British but we have not lived here until yesterday."

"Where did you live then?" the boy asked.

"Just now it was Turkey, though me I was born in Iran," Francesco explained.

"Me I was born in India," said Gussie.

To say these things was too near all they wanted to forget. Anna's voice became a whisper and her eyes filled with tears.

"Me I was the only one not born in the caravan."

The boy was puzzled. If they lived in a caravan they must be gypsies, but they didn't look like gypsies.

"What's your name then? Mine's Wally — well, Walter really, but everyone calls me Wally."

Francesco introduced them.

"Me I am Francesco, this is Gussie and this is Anna."

"Where you living then?"

"In a road called The Crescent," said Gussie. "The house is called Dunroamin and we want a stall to sell some clothes."

"And three suitcases," Anna reminded him.

"Good clothes, Anna's other frock which is blue, and we have flannel shorts and a shirt each," Francesco explained.

To Wally the children seemed as helpless as babies. He knew The Crescent. There were nice houses up there. Not the sort where the owners booked a stall to sell clothes.

"Look 'ere," he said in the voice he would have used to a baby. "Me mum will be back in a minute and she don't fancy people standing round, not unless they're buyin' anythin'. Now there is a seat down there, go and sit on it until I come. You can't 'ave a stall but maybe I'll think of a way round thin's."

Wally did not keep the children waiting long, for he arrived on a rattling old bicycle which was much quicker than using his feet.

"Mum's back," he said, propping his bicycle against the seat. Then he sat down between Francesco and Anna. "Now, let's 'ave the whole boilin'. Why, livin' in The Crescent, do you want to sell your clothes?"

Anna answered.

"Because of me. I must learn to dance."

"Jardek – he was our mother's father – was a very great teacher of dancing in Warsaw and he said Anna has the real special spark," Francesco explained.

Gussie joined in.

"When there is a great gift not to learn is a sin. But The Uncle we now live with says it is to dance that is the sin."

To Wally the children might have come from another planet. He was fascinated by them, and at the same time felt protective about them. He had found them, they were his to look after.

"You got to get one thin' in your 'eads. This is England and in England kids your age can't work, it's against the law. If you was to set up a stall you'd 'ave the coppers after you. Nor you can't 'ave a paper round nor nothin' like that."

Francesco studied Wally. Wally was bigger built than he was but he didn't look much older.

"But you are working. How old are you?"

Wally shook his head sadly at such ignorance.

"I'm ten but I'm not workin', just standin' in for me mum while she had a cuppa. The coppers knows us, they knows it's just on account of it's the school 'olidays, they'd be around all right if I was helping me mum of a term time."

Anna had an idea.

"Do you think it would be possible for our things to be sold on your stall?"

Wally thought about that.

"I'd 'ave to talk to me mum. You see, your uncle might think your clothes was his like, then he would call it stealin'. Me mum wouldn't 'ave nothin' to do with that. 'Ow much money was you wanting?"

"We have these," Francesco showed Wally the tenpenny pieces, "but we want much more for it is for dancing shoes."

"Mine," Anna explained, "were lost in the earthquake with all else."

At that moment the Town Hall clock struck twelve-thirty. The children got up.

"We must go," Francesco explained. "We have to be very punctual or The Uncle will be angry."

Wally could not bear to let them go. They had been fascinating before but now with Anna saying her shoes were lost in an earthquake they were like something on the telly.

"Now look," he said, "I gotta 'ave time to think what's best to be done. Can you be back 'ere by 'alf past two?"

To the children, used to roaming where they would, this presented no difficulties.

"Of course," said Gussie, "we've nothing to do."

Wally watched them walk down the hill. He hated to see them go.

"Watch it now," he called after them, "see you two-thirty."

Sir William had not been at all happy about leaving the children at Fyton. He had taken an instant dislike to Cecil, who seemed to him both prim and smug. He had in the short while he had known them become fond of the children. But what could he do? Without doubt Cecil Docksay was Christopher Docksay's only brother and, therefore, legal guardian to the children. He could not have been said to be exactly welcoming when he met them at the airport, but on the other hand he had not suggested he did not want them. Suppose the children were wretchedly unhappy with their uncle, could anything be done?

Sir William was so worried about the children that he asked an old friend who was a barrister to dinner, and to him poured out his anxieties.

The barrister listened with interest, for he knew about pictures and had admired Christopher Docksay's work.

"I should try and see the children as often as you can. It's about all you can do, unless of course you think they are neglected."

"But there are other forms of neglect besides what is legally meant by the word, aren't there?" Sir William asked. "I mean, the children have lost everyone they loved, they need that replaced."

"You're on a difficult wicket there. Much the best thing you can do is keep in touch. You could see them when you are in England, couldn't you, and write to them when you are away? Children love getting letters."

Sir William had never written to a child in his life. Now he looked in a worried way at his friend.

"Write about what?"

The barrister, who had brought up four children and who now had nine grandchildren, laughed.

"You old bachelor, you. You've had the children with you for over a week, you must have some idea what interests them."

It was then Sir William remembered the talk he had had with the children in Istanbul.

"The girl Anna wants to learn to dance."

"All girls go through that stage," said the barrister. "It doesn't last."

Sir William tried to catch an atmosphere.

"These aren't ordinary children. They have been brought up with a deep respect for art in any form. It seems their maternal grandfather taught dancing in Warsaw. He was teaching the girl whom, according to the children, he thought was the real thing."

"Well, that's a good start for a letter to the children. Ask if they've fixed on a dancing teacher."

"If they haven't, who is the best?"

The barrister thought.

"None of my brood was anywhere near first-class but I remember talk. There is a Madame Scarletti, who must be very old now, but I believe she is still going. Now she was a Pole, she married an Italian called Scarletti. You could find the address of her studio in the telephone book."

9. Hair

THE CRESCENT WAS buzzing with the news. One paper had said Christopher Docksay had left three children. Another had said they had been in hospital but had left for England in the care of Sir William Hoogle. No paper had said the children had been brought to Fyton to live with their uncle, but it had taken no one in The Crescent long to put two and two together. Yesterday children with suitcases had been seen getting out of "that odd Mr Docksay's" car. This morning three children had been seen going out shopping with Mrs Docksay. Many people in The Crescent had children of their own, others had grandchildren, but all, whether they had families or not, said:

"Poor children! We must see what we can do to help."

Cecil Docksay had been working all the morning. Though he had retired from his bank he was still a busy man, for, being good at figures – which is something bank managers have to be – he was in demand to be the treasurer of charities. It could not be said he was liked for he was unsociable, but it was admitted he was useful.

Now, his work over, he was in his garden looking proudly at his plastic flowers when, out of the corner of his eye, he saw what he described to himself as "some fool" in the next garden watering his real flowers. He paid no attention because he was not the sort of man neighbours talked to over garden fences, but that day he had a surprise. The neighbour spoke to him.

"I believe Christopher Docksay was your brother. I'm so sorry. Terrible tragedy. Don't know much about pictures myself but the papers say he was a wonderful artist." Cecil muttered something that just might have been "thank you". "My wife," the neighbour went on, "met three children out with Mrs Docksay this morning. Are they your brother's kids? Saw in the paper there were three coming to England."

Cecil was livid at what he considered inquisitiveness but he had to answer.

"That's right. They're living here."

The neighbour swallowed back the "Heaven help them" which sprang to his lips. Instead he said:

"We were wondering if the children would like to come to tea one day. We've got twins, you know – a boy and a girl. They're eleven."

Cecil was speechless with rage. Ever since they had lived in Dunroamin he and Mabel had kept themselves to themselves.

Now, after one night in the house, the children were being asked out to tea. It was unbearable.

"Not going out at the moment," he growled and strode back into his house and shut the door. At the same time he looked at his watch, three minutes to one, the children had better be punctual or he'd show them who was master here.

There can be few things more annoying when you are feeling cross than that those with whom you are cross should take the wind out of your sails by doing exactly what you had meant to scold them for not doing. Exactly at one o'clock the three children, washed and tidy, walked into the dining room.

The idea was Francesco's. Walking home, he had been thinking about his uncle. Upstairs, he told his thoughts to the others.

"If we take care never to do anything in anger, and if we try not to speak at meals, it will be much better for The Uncle will leave us alone."

"Why should we?" Gussie expostulated. "I like talking at meals like we always have, and if I'm angry I do things at once without thinking."

Anna agreed with Francesco. She had come into the boys' room to have her hair plaited.

"He's quite right, Gussie. It is not nice here but we must try while S'William is in Alaska. When he comes back perhaps he will sell our picture, then something better could be managed."

To add to the tidy washed look Francesco felt was expected of them he tried to do something with Gussie's hair. They all had thick dark hair but Gussie's had a slight curl in his which made it stand up. Francesco, much to Gussie's annoyance, took a wet comb to it.

"Why should I comb my hair to please The Uncle?" he grumbled. "I do not like him so I don't care how it looks. Anyway, it was cut and washed in Istanbul."

On their first day in Istanbul Sir William had sent all three children to a hairdresser.

"You boys look like a couple of savages," he had said, "and Anna is not much better."

"Our hair is usually much better than now," Gussie had told him. "It is the earthquake, it makes a terrible dust."

"Our mother was always washing and cutting our hair," Francesco had added. "For Anna she tied it on top of her head with a ribbon so her neck was cool."

This was so vivid a picture that none of the children could bear to think of it.

Sir William saw this.

"I didn't suppose your hair was always a mess. You must remember I was never in an earthquake. But yours does need washing and perhaps a bit of cutting. What length you wear it is your business, but you might have it trimmed."

But that was a week ago and Gussie's hair, though clean, was on end again. Francesco slicked it down with a wet comb which was unbecoming but effective.

"Now we all wash," he said. "Then we watch over the stairs and the moment The Aunt comes out of the kitchen with the food we walk down the stairs."

Cecil looked at the children to find something about them on which he could rub off his anger. But there was nothing. They were not a credit to him because, having lived so long in hot countries, they were pale compared with ordinary English children, and they had dark circles under their eyes as a result of all they had suffered. Then he noticed Gussie's hair. The wet comb had not only made the hair lie down neatly but also had made it look longer. If there was one thing Cecil hated it was boys with long hair.

"You need your hair cut, Augustus," he said. "You can have it done this afternoon."

Gussie clean forgot what had been decided in the bedroom.

"Cut! Cut! Cut!" he said. "Everybody speaks about cutting. It was cut last week in Istanbul."

Mabel was putting helpings of fish pie on the plates. This meant her back was to the table, but even from that position she could feel a diversion was necessary if Cecil was not to get angry.

"Don't worry, dear," she said to Cecil. "I'll see Gussie goes to the barber's." Then, to keep Gussie quiet, she added: "Would you two boys come and hand round the plates?"

Francesco could see Gussie was longing to go on arguing, so as he gave his uncle his plate of fish pie he asked:

"How much in England is it to have the hair cut?"

"Too much by a long chalk," said Cecil. "Probably twenty-five pence. Everything costs too much these days."

That silenced Gussie. Twenty-five pence would be more

than those ten pences. If only The Aunt did not come with them surely they could find a way to keep the money.

It was lucky the children had had a busy morning for it had made them hungry, so somehow they forced down the fish pie which they all — used to highly seasoned food — thought disgusting. The fish pie was followed by what Mabel called a summer pudding. It was made of bread and blackcurrants and though, as the children agreed later, not nice it was good for taking away the taste of the fish pie. At the end of the meal Cecil put his hand in his pocket and took out some change and passed it over to Francesco.

"There's twenty-five but you may get it done for twenty. If you do, bring me the change. And see Augustus's hair is cut really short, he looks like a girl as he is, and anyway I'm not made of money, this cut had got to last a long time."

Fortunately Mabel had no intention of going with the children to the hairdresser. She told them where the barber's shop was, then she turned her worried mouselike face to Francesco.

"I trust you, dear, to see it really is cut short. You don't want unpleasantness, do you?"

Gussie only waited to get the other two alone before he burst out:

"I do want unpleasantness. I won't have my hair cut. Christopher liked it, Olga liked it and so I think did Jardek and Babka — at least, they never said they didn't. If anyone tries to cut my hair I'll run away."

Francesco and Anna knew that when Gussie got cross he

could talk louder and louder until he was almost screaming.

"You know we can't have your hair cut," said Francesco, "this twenty-five is for Anna's shoes."

"Then what will The Uncle say?" Gussie demanded.

"This I do not know," Francesco admitted. "But we will tell all to Wally and he will find an answer."

10. Wally's Mum

WALLY WAS ALREADY sitting on the seat when the children arrived. This time he had not brought his bicycle. He was so pleased to see them he bounced off the seat and rushed to meet them.

"There you are! You gotta come to me mum's stall. I told 'er how Anna had lost her dancing shoes in the earthquake and she's ever so interested. She says she read about you in the paper, you know, your dad and mum and that being killed. She says you come and talk to 'er an' she's sure thin's can be sorted out so's you've enough for Anna's shoes. What's an earthquake like?"

Francesco did not want Gussie to be sick or Anna to cry so he said:

"I'll tell you some day but just now we want a way to cut Gussie's hair without spending money."

"You see," Anna explained, "The Uncle has given twenty-five pence for it to be cut, but we need the money for my dancing shoes."

Gussie caught hold of Wally's sleeve.

"I don't want it cut. It's all right the way it is. Anyway, I do not like The Uncle so I won't do things to please him."

Wally was not sure how his mother would react to this hair business. She might think taking twenty-five pence, meant for hair cutting, to buy shoes was cheating. So all he said was:

"We'll ask Mum, she'll know what's best."

Wally's mum was waiting for them behind her stall. Her name was Mrs Wall. The children took to her right away. She had red hair like Wally and, though she was not old, she had a fat cosy look. They had not seen anybody fat and cosy since Babka and, now they saw fat and cosiness again, they knew how badly they had missed her.

"This is them," said Wally in a proud voice, rather as if he was introducing three TV stars.

Wally's mum saw the pale faces and the shadows under the eyes and she felt so sorry for the children that it hurt. She pulled Anna to her and gave her a hug.

"So it's you who wants to learn dancin'."

That hug was too much for Anna. It was just the way Babka had hugged. Ever since Sir William had looked after them all three children had tried not to think of things which reminded them of the little house that went away. And most of the time they had succeeded, pushing other things on top of what they were trying to forget. Now, with one hug, Wally's mum had brought everything back. It was like a dam breaking. All the pushed-away hopeless misery came tumbling out. First Anna was crying, then Gussie and finally Francesco.

Wally's mum was a great believer in having a good cry.

"That's right," she said in her warm cosy voice. "No good bottlin' thin's up." Then, over the heads of the three children for by now she had them all in her arms, she called out to Wally:

"Get the stall packed, dear, then we'll go 'ome and I'll make a nice cuppa tea. Nothing like a cuppa when you're feeling low."

The children cried for quite a long time for they had a lot of held-in crying to get out of them. But when they had reached the occasional hiccupping-sob stage Wally's mum said:

"Now, blow your noses and we'll get movin'. Wally's packed the pram."

It had not struck the children to wonder how Wally's mum transported her goods to her stall. They had often watched stalls put up, and knew that at the end of the day someone would come and help carry away the baskets and boxes. Or perhaps a boy would arrive with a donkey. But a perambulator was something new.

"How is it you have the perambulator?" Gussie asked in the sniffy voice of someone who has been crying.

Wally's mum laughed.

"You'd never think it but it's Wally's old pram. His dad said he'd sell it when Wally got past it, but I had a feeling it would come in useful and it has."

"You see, me dad was a lorry driver," Wally explained, "and he was in a smash. Well, he can't do much now so that's why me mum has the stall, and the perambulator's grand for getting the stuff along."

"Wally comes to push the perambulator 'ome after school, he never misses," Wally's mum said proudly.

The boys helped Wally push the perambulator and as they walked the children told Wally's mum about their troubles.

"The Uncle is a terrible man," Gussie explained. "He says to dance is a sin."

Wally's mum, though sorry for the children, still held to her views on what was right.

"Well, the one who pays the piper calls the tune," she said, "and you can't go against that."

"You do not see that I must dance?" Anna asked, appalled.

Wally's mum put an arm around Anna and gave her a squeeze.

"I never said that. Of course you must dance if you 'ave the gift. But this uncle – well, he has taken you in and he's feedin' you and that, so it's his right to say if he don't hold with dancing."

Then they told her about the ice cream ten pences and the twenty-five pence for the hair cutting.

"We do not know how much the shoes will cost," Anna explained, "but forty-five pence must help."

Wally's mum thought about that.

"The tens you were given for the ice cream, that's all right, but I don't know about that twenty-five that was given for hair cuttin' and nothin' else."

"But I won't have it cut," said Gussie. "I like it the way it is, everybody liked it, there is only The Uncle who wants it short."

Wally's mum looked at Gussie with a twinkle in her eye.

"I see I'll 'ave to say to you what I says to Wally – 'want will 'ave to be your master'."

"But, Mum," said Wally, "couldn't Dad…"

His mum silenced him with a gesture.

"We'll see what we'll see. Now come in, dears, and I'll put on the kettle."

They had stopped outside a small house sitting by itself in a field. In the field there were a lot of hens and one cock and a sty from which came the grunting of a pig.

"You have a farm," said Francesco. "We had many friends who had farms."

Wally's mum laughed.

"It's 'ardly a farm but Wally's dad always fancied pig-keepin' and when 'e got compensation for his accident we spent it on this place. 'E can't do much from 'is wheelchair but Wally 'elps and the pig is company for 'is dad when we're out."

"Come on," Wally told the children. "We keeps the pram back of the pigsty. We'll tell Dad we're 'ome."

Wally's dad was in his wheelchair. He seemed to have lost

both legs in his motor accident but he was a very cheerful man.

"Meet our Bess," he said, pointing to the very fat pig in the sty. "Makes a lovely pet Bessie does."

Wally did the honours.

"This is Francesco and this is Gussie and this is Anna, they were in an earthquake."

Wally's dad had also read his newspaper. He gave the children a quick look, then he changed the subject.

"Is your mum making a cuppa then? Looks like we could all do with it."

Over tea and a splendid cake Wally's dad was told about Anna's dancing and the twenty-five pence for Gussie to have his hair cut. That made him look at Gussie.

"Well, you could do with a cut."

"But I don't want it done," Gussie protested, "and we need the money for Anna's shoes. She can't practise properly in socks."

Mr Wall looked at his wife.

"You get out the basin and me scissors."

Wally's mum got up.

"Lovely hair cutter he is. Just amateur like. But there's quite a few come to him."

Wally's dad beamed at Gussie.

"Then you gives me the twenty-five for the 'aircut and I gives it back to you and everybody's 'appy."

"Except me," Gussie growled.

"Even you, I shouldn't wonder," said Wally's dad. "It's a

marvel the way I can keep cuttin' and still leave the 'air looking OK."

Wally's mum put a stool for Gussie beside the wheelchair and wrapped a towel round him, then Mr Wall put a pudding basin on Gussie's head and clipped at the hair that was outside it.

"It's not just the shoes, is it?" Wally's mum asked Anna and Francesco. "Wally was telling me you wanted to sell some clothes."

"They are ours – given us by S'William, so absolutely nothing to do with The Uncle," Gussie shouted.

"You sit still and don't talk," said Mr Wall, "or I'll 'ave a ear off of you."

"We have a suitcase each and Anna has another frock and we have shorts and shirts," Francesco explained. "But we do not know of a teacher so we cannot tell how much it will cost."

Wally's mum looked at Wally.

"Isn't there someone the girls go to of a Saturday?"

Wally nodded.

"Miss Audrey de Veane. Lovely teacher they say she is."

"Puts on shows for charity and that, doesn't she?" his mother asked.

"Them as is old enough gets work in pantomimes," said Wally. "Wouldn't fancy it meself, but she's well spoke of."

"You know any girl what learns off of 'er?"

Wally sighed.

"Well, that Doreen does, you know – her down by the

church. Silly sort she is but she does learn the dancing."

"You'll go on your bike first thing tomorrow. Just ask her what this Miss de Veane charges. No need to tell her why – just ask."

The children had to go home soon after that. Gussie's hair was finished, it looked rather peculiar for it was much shorter at the back than at the front, though there was still a lot on the top of his head.

"Aren't they lovely people?" Francesco said.

Gussie skipped on ahead.

"Wouldn't it be good if we could live there instead of with The Uncle?"

Francesco felt the twenty-five pence in his pocket.

"And what a day! We have more money for the shoes. We have found someone who teaches dancing and Wally's mum will sell what we need to pay her. Are you pleased, Anna?"

Anna hesitated.

"Yes. Of course I am glad if the lady can teach as Jardek did. But until I know that I cannot say if I will learn with her." She looked anxiously at Francesco. "Will you explain this to Wally's mum? I would rather die than she should think I am not grateful."

Francesco sighed. There was so much he had to do now he was head of the family.

"Do not worry," he told Anna. "If you cannot learn from this lady it is I who will explain."

11. Suitcases

THE SHOES ANNA needed would cost £1.40. The children went to a shoe shop to find out. The lady in the shop offered to order the shoes right away but Francesco would not allow that.

"No, first we will pay then you will order."

Outside the shop Gussie and Anna started to argue.

"I wish you'd have let her order," Anna said, "because we know how we will get the money, and I do need the shoes."

"I thought it was silly," Gussie agreed, "for we'll most likely have the money tonight if we give Wally's mum our things to sell today."

Francesco did not answer at once for he was making a plan. It was odd, he thought, how, now he had to be the one to make decisions, he was learning just to make them and did not mind what the other two said.

That day was a good one for getting the things they had

to sell to Wally's mum, for it was a day when Uncle Cecil had to go to London for a meeting.

"Today," said Francesco, "we will only take the suitcases to sell."

"Why only suitcases?" asked Gussie. "With The Uncle out we can take everything. Even if The Aunt saw us I don't think she'd say anything, and anyway they are ours."

"No, just the suitcases," said Francesco. "Those we could not need for we are not going away and, if we did go away, we could use a box, but our clothes we do need. Already The Aunt has washed them, it will be easier if we do not need to sell the clothes."

"If we need more money," Anna suggested, "it may be difficult to take the clothes. Today they could travel in the suitcases."

Francesco thought they were being very stupid.

"But, don't you see, if we sell the clothes and then do not need the money, The Uncle cannot be given the money so he has to spend his money on our clothes. Well, we do not want this for as soon as S'William is home he will sell our picture, then we can pay."

"Oh, very well," said Gussie. "Come on, let's get the suitcases."

Always when Cecil went to London Mabel turned out the house. So when the children ran upstairs to fetch their cases the boys were horrified to find her in their bedroom. She was wearing a big apron and had her hair tied up in a tea cloth. She was polishing the floor with a hairy thing on the end of a long stick. The boys had made their beds and left the room, as they thought, reasonably tidy before they went out, so they saw no need for her presence.

"Let me do that," Gussie said, trying to take the polisher from her.

"We always have helped clean since we were very little," Francesco explained.

Mabel looked more like a frightened mouse than usual. When she spoke she seemed terribly out of breath.

"I haven't touched anything. I have left the envelope under the paper."

Francesco thought he would try and explain.

"It is only S'William's address. We thought that was a safe place."

"It is safe," Mabel puffed. "I shall never touch it or say it is there." She gave a nervous smile. "There is no need to be afraid of me, dears."

Mabel looked as if she was going to say more, but at that second Anna came into the room carrying her suitcase.

It was a horrid moment for nobody knew what to say. Anna stared at Mabel as if she had turned into a dragon. Mabel gazed at the suitcase as if hypnotized. The boys just stood, both trying to think of some reason why Anna was carrying her suitcase.

"We thought..." Francesco began.

"Well, it's always useful to have a case with you," Gussie said in a rush. "You know, to put things in."

Then Mabel surprised them. She leant her polisher against

the wall and sat down on Francesco's bed. She had great difficulty pushing out her words.

"Your uncle is a fine man but he likes to be alone, he does not want strangers in his house."

"I wouldn't call two nephews and a niece strangers," said Gussie.

Mabel went on as if he had not spoken.

"For me your uncle always comes first, but when I can help you I will. We must work together to keep things peaceful. I do not interfere. If you wish to take out a suitcase that is nothing to me."

Francesco thought The Aunt's candour deserved candour in return.

"Really we are taking all three. It's to sell, you see we need money for something."

"Much money?" Mabel asked.

"To us a lot," said Gussie. "We've got forty-five pence but we need one pound and forty pence."

Mabel seemed so reasonable Francesco was beginning to wonder if they should tell her more, but evidently that was not what she wanted for suddenly she got up, picked up her polisher and darted out of the room.

Gussie looked after her in astonishment.

"Did you see? It was just as if she was a mouse and a cat was after her."

Francesco took the suitcases out of the cupboard. He gave Gussie his.

"Come on, let's take them to Wally's mum."

"Of course," said Gussie when they reached the road, "we have never known an aunt. Do you suppose they are all like that?"

"Perhaps British ones," Anna suggested.

Francesco felt somehow better inside because of what Mabel had said.

"It is not the way it was with us – I mean, before the earthquake, where everybody said everything they thought, but I think for her it was a lot, almost I think she meant she was a friend."

Gussie refused to change his view of Mabel.

"To me she is just a mouse. She'd never be a friend. If The Uncle is angry, like a mouse she'd run into her hole."

Anna had put her hand into Francesco's.

"I agree with you. Anyway, for us who have almost no friends, it is nice to have a mouse."

Wally was on the lookout for them. He rushed to meet them.

"I thought you were never coming." He looked admiringly at the suitcases. "Cor! They're a bit of all right, aren't they?"

Wally's mum was serving a customer but she gave the children a gorgeous smile.

"Shan't be long," she called out. "Wally's got something to tell you."

"I almost forgot," said Wally. "That Doreen, her that goes dancing of a Saturday. Well, that Miss de Veane, she charges two pounds and ten pence for a term and there's extra when you take an exam. The term begins when school does and that's the week after next, so you did orter take Anna long to see 'er right away."

Wally's mum was thrilled with the suitcases.

"Now, let's see 'ow much you need and let's see if we can get it."

Francesco held up three fingers.

"Ninety-five pence for the shoes and two pounds and ten pence for the lessons, that's three pounds and five pence altogether."

" 'Ark at you!" said Wally's mum. "Proper adder you are, I was always shockin' at sums and this decimal money drives me up the wall. Give me back the old 'alf crown, that's what I say."

Gussie was not going to allow Francesco to get all the praise.

"We can all add. Olga taught us."

Wally's mum examined the suitcases.

"We did ought to work for a bit over for there may be postage on the shoes and ribbons and that. Suppose I was to try for one pound twenty-five for each? It would give us a nice bit in 'and."

"But we gotta sell 'em, Mum," Wally reminded her. "I mean, Anna can't wait about, that Doreen said she orter see the dancin' teacher right away, and she can't do that not without she's got some shoes."

Wally's mum opened her purse and took out a pound note.

"Go an' order them," she said. "When I says I can sell somethin' I can sell it."

Gussie and Wally took Anna to the shoe shop to order her shoes. Francesco stayed behind to explain to Wally's mum that Anna would not learn from Audrey de Veane if she was not as good as Jardek.

"It could be," he said, "that this Miss de Veane is not what Anna is needing. You see, Jardek was a wonderful teacher."

Wally's mum was making room for the suitcases on her stall.

"Who was this Jardek?"

"The father of our mother."

"Oh, your grandpa. Well, I never knew a grandpa in the dancing line, but I wouldn't suppose 'e'd be better than a lady brought up to it like, would you?"

Francesco screwed up his face, trying to find a way to explain.

"Only Anna will know. So if Anna says she cannot learn from this lady you will not think she is not grateful?"

Wally's mum put a hand on his shoulder.

"Look, son, there's things you've got to understand. This Audrey de Veane is the only one that teaches here."

"But there could be others in some other place."

Wally's mum turned Francesco so that he faced her.

"Not in Fyton there isn't, so Anna, as thin's are, has to learn in Fyton."

"Why?"

"Because that's where the school is. I know you ain't lived

in England and so don't know what's what. But you can take it from me that not you, nor Anna, nor Gussie – not even the Queen 'erself, can alter the school laws. Come the week after next you 'ave to go to school. So it's Miss de Veane of a Saturday for Anna or no dancin' and that's flat."

12. Miss Audrey de Veane

Sir William, when he was a child, had been a keen stamp collector, so he decided the children probably were too, so he wrote to them on the aeroplane. It never crossed his mind there was any urgency. He thought the chances were that there was an established dancing teacher near Fyton and quite possibly Anna's lessons were already arranged. So he wrote the children a friendly letter telling them that he would not be away long, and that when he came back he would ask permission from their uncle to take them out. At the end of the letter he said:

> *If, Anna, you are not fixed up with a suitable dancing teacher I hear very good accounts of a Madame Scarletti. I looked her up in the telephone book. She has a studio at 45 Bemberton Street, Chelsea, London. I gather she is very old but still one of the best teachers in the world.*

Then Sir William licked up the letter, put it in his pocket to post on arrival and forgot all about it for the next six weeks, when by chance he wore that coat again and found the letter in a pocket.

Wally's mum got £1.25 for each suitcase and Wally arranged that Doreen, who lived by the church, should take Anna to Miss de Veane's studio.

"She's a right silly type, that Doreen," he told the children. "Giggles at nothin', but she's been with Miss de Veane since she was ever so small, so she's in with her like so could get her to see Anna."

This was not at all what Anna wanted.

"But it's I who wish to see Miss de Veane. Until I see how she teaches I do not know if it is with her I wish to learn."

"But, Anna," Francesco pleaded, "if she is the only one could you not learn from her just until S'William comes home?"

"I think it is what Jardek would have wished," said Gussie. "Great harm cannot come from one lesson each Saturday."

Anna stamped her foot she was so cross.

"Great harm can come. Wrong positions, wrong use of muscles and my legs may be ruined for ever and ever."

Gussie shrugged and turned to Francesco.

"I do not know why we sold the suitcases. Wally's mum says all must go to school or The Uncle may go to prison. This would I think be a good idea but he will not wish to go. So Anna can only dance when there is no school and there is only one to teach. What more can we do? In London perhaps there are many who teach well but how can Anna go to London? The Uncle will not take her in his car for he thinks to dance is a sin."

Francesco agreed.

"He's quite right, Anna, it's Miss de Veane or nobody at all. Go and see the lady and if she will teach you then try how it goes."

"But if it goes wrong?" said Anna. "She will have all the money for our suitcases, and we have no more money."

"If we must we will get more," Gussie promised, "but go in hope that this lady is such a one as Jardek would approve."

So two days later the boys took Anna, with her shoes in a paper bag – which Mabel gave her without asking why she wanted it – to the house by the church where Doreen lived.

Wally was quite right. Doreen was a very giggling girl, but she was kind-hearted so took complete charge of Anna.

"Now you don't want to be nervous like, she's ever so kind really." Then Doreen giggled. "Course it's different for me, I been with her ever so long so I dance solos and that for her shows."

Doreen was a plump little girl with brown ringlets. She did not, Anna thought, look a dancer, at least she did not look like the girls Jardek had taught of whom he had shown her photographs.

"Which solos do you dance?"

Doreen giggled again.

"All sorts, ever so pretty the costumes I've worn. Once I was a fairy and another time a butterfly and another time the spirit of winter. I wore a big white bonnet for that with a robin on it. Of course mostly it's musical comedy or tap that I do."

Anna had no idea what Doreen was talking about, but it didn't sound the sort of dancing Jardek taught.

The studio door was opened by Miss de Veane. She was a long thin woman with orange-coloured hair which at the roots showed it was really dark. She wore a very tight-fitting black dress and white boots. Anna, as she had been taught to do by Olga to any grown-up, dropped a polite little curtsey.

This made Doreen giggle.

"She's part foreign. That's why she does that, she does it to everyone."

Miss de Veane, perhaps because she had called out orders at dancing classes for so long, had an oddly hoarse voice.

"Very nice, too, I wish you'd all curtsey. I had to when I was a student. Come into the studio. Sit down, Doreen, and try not to giggle. Come here, child. Now put on your shoes."

"Yes, Madame," said Anna.

She sat on the floor and put on her pink canvas shoes on to which Wally's mum had sewn pink ribbons.

"I have a gramophone," Miss de Veane said. "Could you dance to some little thing to show me what you can do?"

Anna looked shocked.

"I was not allowed to do anything but exercises, Madame."

Miss de Veane looked at Anna's tightly plaited hair, her pale heart-shaped face, at the plain but well-cut blue cotton frock she was wearing – an unusual child and, remembering the curtsey, she wondered. Surely in this Fyton into which she had drifted she had not been sent a dancer? Well, even if she had it was too late now, she had lost interest.

"All right," she agreed, "go to the barre. We will start with six demi-pliés."

For ten minutes Miss de Veane rapped out orders, some for exercises at the barre, some to be done in the middle of the room. They were simple enough, such as she taught to those of her girls who wanted to enter for exams. But Anna was younger. When she had finished with her she asked:

"How old are you?"

"Eight, Madame."

Miss de Veane noticed the "Madame" and the foreign accent.

"And your name?"

"Anna Docksay."

"Well, Anna, I will take you as a pupil. My class is at ten on Saturday mornings, that is, tap and ballet. I teach musical comedy to the juniors on Thursday evenings but that's extra."

Anna had not properly understood.

"I only wish for a class for ballet exercises. So I do not make faults which could remain."

Audrey de Veane thought back to her childhood when she had been a promising child dancer. Goodness knows where she might have risen to if she had been carefully trained. But she had been forced through every type of dancing until at twelve she was old enough to join a troupe.

Why should this child be picked out for special attention? *She* had never been. Then something stirred in her, a flicker of the old ambition, even if she herself was past dancing she could at least train a good dancer.

"I do take a few special pupils, usually to coach for a public performance. But I suppose I might squeeze you in. Each lesson will cost fifty pence for half an hour."

Anna had not been in England long enough to be good at understanding the money. She looked anxiously over her shoulder at Doreen who had taken in every word of the conversation. Doreen got up and joined Anna and Miss de Veane.

"That means you could have about four lessons private for what it would cost for a whole term," she explained to Anna.

Anna did not know what to do. Four lessons was very little, but four like the ten minutes she had just done was better than a class which was not all ballet but was also this something that Madame called tap. Among the many things that Jardek had told Anna in mixed Polish and English was that a dancer must live for nothing but dancing, that anything which came between a dancer and dancing must be forgotten absolutely. Anna saw now what Jardek had meant, that after the four lessons were over how to find the fifty pence each week was a thing she must forget entirely. She must trust in God and it would come.

"Thank you, Madame," Anna said firmly. "I think it best I have the private lessons."

13. Twins

NOBODY COULD SETTLE down in Dunroamin, it wasn't that sort of house, but while Anna was with Miss de Veane the boys for the first time since they had arrived had time to look round and see where they had come to live.

When they first realized that there was nothing they had to do they felt they must have forgotten something. But going over things in their bedroom they found they had not. Anna had got her shoes. At this minute they were on her feet. Enough money had been made when Wally's mum sold the suitcases for a whole term's dancing lessons to be paid for.

"It seemed as if there was a lot to do," Francesco explained to Gussie, "because everything took so long. I mean, there was four days between taking Anna to the shop to be measured for shoes and them coming."

"And what a four days," Gussie groaned. "With eating all

that terrible food and my hair being cut."

"I never have known why The Uncle didn't get angry about your hair. Of course it had to be because we needed the twenty-five pence but, though I know Wally's dad tried, it certainly does look most peculiar."

"A crying scandal," Gussie agreed. This was an expression of Christopher's which his family had adopted.

"Yet The Uncle, though he frowned and made snorting noises, said nothing – nothing at all," Francesco marvelled.

Gussie had an idea about this.

"I think that was because, if he didn't like it, the only thing he could do was to pay again and this he will not do. I think he is one with a closed purse."

"Perhaps he is poor," Francesco suggested.

This made Gussie laugh so much that he rolled on his bed.

"Poor! In India, Pakistan, Iran, Iraq, Ethiopia, Egypt – every place we have seen poor. Poor is to swell in the wrong places, to seek for scraps from the gutter, to beg. It is not to eat three meals a day sitting at a table in a good blue suit with a clean starched shirt and have a motorcar in the garage."

"Perhaps there is two kinds of poor," Francesco suggested. "The Uncle has perhaps enough for him and The Aunt but not for the three of us."

Gussie made a rude noise.

"He has a closed purse and I dislike him very much and he eats terrible food."

Francesco sighed.

"Cabbage – that is a dreadful vegetable."

Gussie shuddered.

"Cooked to taste like dirty water. No garlic, no curry – all food here is as if eating paper. But perhaps, because it is never hot in Britain, I am getting hungry like we were before the earthquake so, however bad the food, I now eat."

Francesco had moved to the window.

"I'm beginning to too and so is Anna. Do you know we have been here five days and never gone into the garden."

Gussie joined him and stared admiringly at the gnomes.

"Those are elegant. I never before saw statues painted red. I wonder what it is for which those little men fish."

"We'll look," said Francesco. "The Uncle is gone."

The boys ran down the stairs and went into the lounge. They had not seen this room before because it was in there that Cecil worked. They were spellbound by the sight of it.

"Velvet like in a palace," Francesco gasped. "Imagine sitting every day on green velvet."

Gussie examined the ivy climbing up the trellis work on the wallpaper.

"And such beautiful paper on the walls. It is good we cannot come in here unless The Uncle is out. It would be terrible if we made a dirty mark on such a wall."

There were French windows through to the garden so the boys stepped out and at once saw what a strange garden it was. Not that they had ever owned a garden themselves but they had seen the gardens of others, so they knew what to expect.

"Nothing is real," Gussie exclaimed. "Feel this rose, it is made of stuff like clothes."

Francesco was stroking a plastic spray of orange-coloured climbing nasturtiums.

"Do you remember that Christopher said there were no gardens in the world so beautiful as the gardens of England? This must be what he meant."

Gussie was for once almost speechless he was so full of admiration.

"Such an ideal! No flower ever dies."

"No earth anywhere at all," Francesco marvelled. "You could be all day in such a garden and be as clean as when you started."

"Hi!" said two voices. The boys spun round, and over the wall they saw two faces looking at them – a boy and a girl. Both had blue eyes and straight fair hair.

"Hi!" they replied.

"We are twins," the boy said. "We're Jonathan and Priscilla Allan."

"We are Francesco and Gussie Docksay."

"We know," said Priscilla. "We read about you in the paper. My father asked your uncle if you could come to tea with us."

"I am sorry, we did not know," Francesco apologized. "The Uncle does not talk much."

"Is he better when you know him?" Priscilla asked. "We think he's horrible."

"That's what I think," said Gussie. "We may not speak at

meals unless it is important or uplifting."

Jonathan giggled.

"If we had a rule like that in our house nobody would ever speak at all."

"That is how it is with us," Gussie agreed. "Nobody does speak at all. It is not nice. Before we came here everyone talked mostly all at once."

"Could you come to tea today?" Priscilla asked.

Francesco shook his head.

"Today our sister Anna goes to Miss de Veane to see if she wishes to learn from her, then we go to tell Wally's mum what has happened as she sold our suitcases to pay for her lessons. She always gives us tea when we go there."

"Miss de Veane's all right," said Priscilla. "I go to her on Saturdays. Why did you have to sell your suitcases? Wouldn't your uncle pay for your sister to learn?"

"He thinks to dance is sinful," Francesco explained.

"And I think he does not like to spend money," Gussie added.

"Well, he'll have to spend some soon," said Jonathan. "I suppose you're going to school, aren't you?"

"In the week after this," Francesco agreed.

"Then you'll need uniform," Priscilla told them. "Grey skirts for us girls and shorts for the boys and purple blazers. You've got the shorts but you'll need blazers."

Francesco and Gussie looked at each other.

"There has been no talk of clothes," said Gussie. "Do all have to wear this?"

"I don't think they can make you," said Priscilla. "But you'll look pretty odd if you don't for everyone does."

"I think this we should tell The Aunt," Francesco told Gussie, then he remembered his manners. "Thank you for asking us to tea, but we do not know if it is possible. The Uncle does not seem to know people."

"Then come tomorrow," said Priscilla, "and we'll get the gang along, there's lots of us in The Crescent."

Cecil was still out so the boys rushed into the kitchen where Mabel was making a cottage pie for lunch.

"Next door," said Gussie, "there are twins called Jonathan and Priscilla and they say we have to have uniform for the school."

"The grey shorts we have," said Francesco, "but we have to wear something purple, I do not know what."

"And Anna will need a grey skirt."

Mabel left the pie and sank on to a chair.

"Uniform?" she panted. "Yes, all the children here wear it. Grey with purple blazers. Oh dear, I suppose I should speak to your uncle."

Francesco felt sorry for Mabel for she was so obviously scared.

"If there is no money for the uniform I do not think it matters. Priscilla did not think we must wear it only we would look" – he turned to Gussie – "how did she say?"

"Pretty odd," said Gussie, "if we didn't, but we don't mind looking odd if there is no money."

Mabel made several efforts to get her words out.

"It's not that there's no money," she explained at last, "but your uncle feels it should be used for promoting special causes, you know he has special causes? He's very generous to them."

To the boys nothing could matter less than what clothes they wore. Francesco, feeling Mabel was still looking fussed, gave her arm a friendly pat.

"Forget the uniform. It is not nice for The Uncle to have us when he does not want us. It is better we do not aggravate."

Mabel seemed as if from somewhere she was getting courage. There was pink in her cheeks and her voice was stronger than usual.

"Your uncle doesn't know about this so you mustn't say anything, but I have some savings and there is money from the State. It's very wrong of me to have savings without telling him, but there it is – I have them. So leave it to me, by the time school starts you'll all be wearing uniforms."

14. Neighbours

THE BOYS SAW Anna coming home and went to the gate to meet her. Her news was not what they wanted to hear. It had been almost like old times to wander where they fancied, talking to whom they fancied without having Anna's dancing lessons or dancing shoes or the ribbon for the shoes to worry about. So when she came home and told them what she had arranged Gussie couldn't control his disgust.

"All that money for just four lessons! Then fifty pence wanted each week!" He slid to the ground and lay flat on his back. "Just thinking of it exhausts me."

Francesco pulled Gussie to his feet.

"Will you never learn? In Britain nobody lies down in the street. And outside the house of The Uncle!" Then he turned to Anna. Where dancing was concerned he trusted her absolutely so if she had said she must have private lessons, private lessons – bad news though it was – it had to be. "We must talk to Wally and his father and mother, they will know how a child earns money in England."

"Could it not be," Anna suggested, "that after four weeks S'William is home? Then he will sell the picture."

"We will of course write," Francesco agreed, "but we must make plans in case he does not arrive."

That afternoon they went as arranged to what they called Wally's farm. By now they were on patting terms with Bess, the pig, but they were making no headway with the hens and the cock.

"I wish they would like us," Anna said. "When you have few friends even a hen can be a comfort."

Wally's mum heard them coming.

"Come along in, dears. Well, Anna, will Miss de Veane 'ave you?"

The family were sitting round the table on which were the tea things and a cake. There were three empty chairs waiting for the children. Gussie drew one to the table and sat down.

"She would have," he said, "but Anna thinks it better she should have private lessons."

Wally and his mum and dad gazed at Anna as if she were the Loch Ness monster. Each was thinking of what trouble everyone had taken to get the shoes and raise the money for the term's classes, and here was Anna saying she needed private lessons.

"Private lessons!" said Wally's mum. "Won't they be pricey?"

Gussie accepted a slice of cake from Wally's dad. He nodded.

"Fifty new pence for one half-hour each Wednesday after school."

"This means," Francesco explained, "we have money enough for five lessons so Gussie and I we must earn this money each week."

Gussie took the cup of tea Wally's mum passed to him.

"In Britain no one has a donkey to load or a camel to lead, nor a store to mind while they sleep."

Wally, Wally's dad and Wally's mum were all shocked that a child of Anna's age should think she needed private dancing lessons at the terrible price of fifty pence for half an hour each week. But they knew the boys were fussing about Anna learning to dance so they spoke cautiously.

"I suppose," Wally's mum suggested, "you couldn't try the Saturday morning class for just one term, could you, Anna?"

Anna turned her big dark eyes to Wally's mum.

"Miss de Veane said things right. Six demi-pliés in each position. But my shoes are new so in the fifth position my shoe slipped so my foot is not turned out right. And at once the Madame said: 'Watch that back foot.' That is how Jardek would speak but not of course in English words. In a big class the Madame cannot watch every foot so it is better one half hour alone, then I work in my bedroom on the other days. Then if faults come she will see at my next lesson."

As far as Wally and his mum and dad were concerned Anna might have been speaking in a foreign language. But evidently Francesco and Gussie understood.

"So you see," Gussie said, "these private lessons is how it must be."

"And they cannot stop after five lessons," Francesco added, "so we must always earn the money."

Gussie turned to Francesco.

"I have an idea. If we could borrow some old, very poor clothes we could beg." He held up both hands and whined: "Alms for the love of Allah."

Wally's dad laughed.

"You do that, son, and you'll find the police after you. Nobody can't beg in this country."

"Not real beggin'," Wally's mum explained. "There's some way of getting a licence to sell matches and such like."

"But you wouldn't get a licence," said Wally. "You're too young."

Gussie sighed.

"It is a pity. I have seen many beg so I know how this is done."

To Wally the children were still something out of a fairy tale. So if Anna had to have fifty new pence every week – scandalous waste of money though it seemed to him – she had to have it.

"Don't worry," he said. "I'll 'ave a word with some of the boys, maybe they'll know of a way."

Wally's dad, during his years as a lorry driver, had known of many methods by which money was made – sometimes by children – which he thought odd if not downright dishonest. These children who had lived such a strange roving life ought to have an eye kept on them, especially young Gussie who was, he thought, less sensible than the other two.

"Tell you what, if Wally can hear of anything you could do decent, like weeding a garden or cleanin' a car then it's OK, but anythin' out of the ordinary you come to me. We don't want you gettin' into any trouble, do we?"

The journey to London seemed to have given Uncle Cecil time to think, or perhaps at his meeting he had met a stodgy friend who had encouraged him by thinking the same as he did, for that night after supper he said:

"I wish to talk to you three. Come into the lounge."

Even Gussie quailed. Clearly The Uncle had found out they had sold the suitcases and what he would do was past imagining. To add to Gussie's troubles the food that night seemed to them all particularly revolting. A reddish sort of meat with yellow fat served with balls made of what the children thought was a form of blanket. There was also cabbage. Gussie, after a few mouthfuls, had leant towards Mabel.

"Always I am eating," he whispered to Mabel, "what I do not like, but this is impossible."

Mabel, gasping and puffing, had whispered back:

"It's boiled silverside and dumplings, dear. It is a great favourite of your uncle's."

Gussie, who believed he would be poisoned if he ate what was on his plate, turned thankfully to his uncle and pushed his plate towards him.

"You like it. You have it. For me, if it is possible, I would like bread and butter and olives."

From the way the uncle and aunt stared at Gussie he might have asked him for some extravagant dainty instead of for the simplest food of which he knew.

At last, after a terrible pause, Uncle Cecil said in a voice like the inside of a refrigerator:

"Take away his plate, Mabel. Augustus will eat nothing tonight."

So it was with their hearts in their mouths that the three children followed Uncle Cecil into the lounge and sat down facing him on the sofa. Anna, scared though she was, had to smile when she felt the sofa.

"At what are you smiling, Anna?" her uncle demanded.

Anna stopped smiling.

"It is this so beautiful sofa," she whispered. "I do not think I have sat on velvet before."

Uncle Cecil did not seem interested.

"I shall pass over your ill-behaviour, Augustus, in not eating your dinner," he said. "Your punishment is that you will go to bed hungry. What I wish to talk to you about is my neighbours. When we first settled here we decided, your aunt and I, to keep ourselves to ourselves. We had no wish to waste time on idle gossip. So the same rule will apply to you. You will meet the local children at school but your friendship will finish there. You will not go inside their homes and of course you will never invite any of them here."

Francesco thought of Jonathan and Priscilla.

"There are twins who live on the other side of the wall. They were asking us to tea."

"You will say no," said Uncle Cecil.

Gussie felt, as he was in disgrace already, a little more wouldn't hurt.

"Why can't we go to tea?"

Uncle Cecil looked at Gussie and that he disliked him showed.

"Because your English is atrocious. When the term starts with school and homework plus a lesson in English from me, when I am free, your days will be full. I do not want you wasting your time and injuring your eyesight staring at television and chattering with the neighbourhood children."

The children had never seen television. There was a set at Wally's farm but it was never turned on when they were there so it meant nothing to them. But they had always talked to everybody they met as best they could in their mixed languages, so they were incapable of believing their uncle meant what he said or, if he did, that it would really happen. People always talked to each other. What really mattered in this conversation was the awful news that Uncle Cecil intended to teach them English. That was terrifying. And when? Would it interfere with Anna's dancing lessons? However, nothing could be done that night so Francesco got up. He bowed to his uncle.

"Thank you for telling us," he said politely.

Gussie gave less of a bow and spoke in rather a growly voice.

"Thank you."

Anna gave her little bob curtsey.

"Thank you, Uncle Cecil. Good night."

But outside the lounge when the door was shut Gussie made a rude face at it.

"And I shan't go hungry to bed. The Aunt will see I eat."

And Gussie was quite right. There was a splendid cheese sandwich under his pillow.

15. What The Uncle Thinks

THE NEXT MORNING after breakfast Francesco followed Aunt Mabel into her kitchen. Each time he saw the kitchen he was filled with fresh admiration. There had not really been a kitchen in the caravan for the stove on which the food was cooked was usually put outside. In Jardek and Babka's little house the kitchen had been a very small sort of outhouse. He gave a great satisfied sigh.

"This room is beautiful," he told Mabel. "Almost too good for using."

Mabel in bed the night before had worried about the children's food. It was true they were eating better but she could see they seldom liked what she cooked.

"What sort of food did you eat when... well, I mean, before the earthquake?" she puffed.

Francesco tried to remember.

"Nothing had a name, there was much stews and rice and all is tasting very good with garlic, and often there is a curry so hot it makes tears in the eyes and…"

Mabel gasped as if she was tasting the curry.

"I'm afraid your uncle wouldn't like that sort of food at all."

"If perhaps some food might be left on the plate," Francesco suggested. "That is a terrible thing that cabbage."

"Next time your uncle goes to London," Mabel whispered, "we will have mushrooms. You'll like those."

Francesco remembered why he was there.

"The Uncle says we may not talk to the children who live next door but they were asking us to tea. Since we may not speak have you perhaps a piece of paper and an envelope so we may write to explain why?"

Aunt Mabel, who had been washing up, stopped and went to sit in a chair. She pointed to the door.

"Shut that please." Francesco shut the door and Aunt Mabel pointed to another chair. "Sit down, there, dear. I want to try and make you understand something." Francesco sat and Aunt Mabel, very puffily, went on. "You uncle is a good man but he does not like children, so it's hard for him that you are here, but he does his duty – he gives you a home."

"We did not ask to come," Francesco reminded her.

"I know," Aunt Mabel agreed, "and I am very glad you are here. But for your uncle it is different. You see, though he was working when your father went away and he was told by your grandfather that he was…" she broke off unable to finish.

Francesco was totally unembarrassed, so often he had

heard his father roaring with laughter describing his escape from England so that he could paint. He tried to put his aunt at ease.

"Christopher's father said he stole but all he took was enough to sell to take him to Paris where he must paint. Some day he knew he would have money and when that day came, of his share he must lose what he had taken. This is not to steal, it is to borrow, that is all."

Aunt Mabel nodded.

"Yes, dear, but your uncle does not see it like that. He was brought up to believe his brother was a thief. So now he feels it is necessary to take special care of you three so nothing bad can influence you. That is really why you may not know the local children, you see you might watch something unsuitable on the television. You know, Westerns and things like that."

Francesco had no idea what a Western was, but what his aunt had said had set up a little worry in his mind. If just borrowing enough things to sell to pay your fare to Paris was something that in Britain made you a thief, perhaps special care should be taken of Gussie who was in so many ways so like Christopher. Care too should perhaps be taken of Anna who, if money was needed for dancing lessons, might take anything. But those were not thoughts with which to trouble The Aunt.

"I understand and I will make the others understand. Now perhaps I could have the paper and the envelope?"

Aunt Mabel opened a drawer in the dresser and showed him notepaper and envelopes. Then she picked up a little box.

"And if you should ever want to write a letter that needs stamps, I keep them in here."

The letter was the work of all three children. They wrote it lying on the floor in Anna's bedroom. Francesco did the writing prompted by Gussie and Anna, all remembering carefully Olga's lessons on letter writing and how the difficult words should be spelt.

My dear Twins – they had to put that for they had no idea how to spell Jonathan and Priscilla – *we send you greetings. We regret we cannot accept your kind invitation for The Uncle wishes us to study for we speak English very bad but we shall meet you at school with sincere felicitations. Francesco. Gussie. Anna.*

The next question was how the letter should be delivered.

"I think we should fix it to a stone and throw it over the wall," Gussie suggested.

"That cannot be," Francesco pointed out. "The Uncle sits in the lounge and he will see. No, one of us must go to the house and knock."

"To knock we need not," said Anna. "In Britain all houses have a slit in the door for letter, and like here there is always a bell."

In the end it was decided Anna should take the letter.

"But do not ring the bell," Francesco told her. "Go soft as a little cat to the house and just put it through the slit in the door."

Anna, though secretly scared in case The Uncle saw her, carried out her mission successfully and the envelope lay safely on the next door house's mat.

That afternoon was Anna's first dancing lesson. Francesco and Gussie took her to the studio for Wally's mum thought she should not walk about on her own. At the studio door, Francesco gave Anna the fifty pence for her lesson.

"Try and make her write down you have paid in case she asks twice," he said, "for fifty pence is a lot of money."

Miss de Veane was alone when Anna arrived. Anna gave her little bob and handed over the fifty-pence piece.

"Here is the money, Madame."

Audrey de Veane gazed down at Anna and felt a curious sensation, it was a feeling of tenderness, which she did not recognize for it was so many years since she had felt it. She had looked not unlike this little girl once. But hard times and the need to work had soon knocked sense into her. Then she had married and come to live in Fyton where she had thought to live as an ordinary housewife for the rest of her days. It was not to be, her husband had died leaving her a house but very little money, so she had earned what she needed in the only way she knew – teaching dancing. Even in Fyton she supposed there might be somebody worth teaching. But there never had been. What she had taught was a long line of Doreens, all giggles and curls without as much talent as would fill a saltspoon. Then out of the blue had come this child. Was it possible? Then she gave herself a mental shake. She must be getting soppy in her old age, she told herself.

"Thank you, Anna," she said putting away the fifty-pence piece. "Now put on your shoes while I write out the receipt."

By now, through gossip and the papers, she knew who Anna was. "Whom do I make it out to? Your uncle?"

Anna, bent over her shoes, kept her head.

"No. Mr Francesco Docksay."

Outside the boys waited, leaning against the wall.

"One lesson gone," said Francesco, "and only four left and still it is we do not know how it is we may earn fifty pence each week."

"Perhaps," Gussie suggested, "Anna is not liking Miss de Veane. Then we must wait until S'William comes home and can sell the picture and tell us where it is Anna should learn."

Francesco looked sadly down the road.

"If only in Fyton there was donkeys and camels to be watched or messages to run. But here there is nothing, all is ordered and arranged."

Gussie slid to the ground and stretched out flat on the pavement.

"All is too honest here, you cannot bargain in the shops, so how can you make a little money on the side?"

Francesco caught hold of Gussie by his jersey.

"Get up. Each day I am telling you on the streets in Britain, you cannot lie."

Gussie sat up.

"Why not? Why should I stand for half an hour? I was in nobody's way."

Francesco pulled Gussie to his feet.

"I do not know why but I do know care should be taken. Today I am talking to The Aunt and she is saying The Uncle is believing Christopher was a thief."

Gussie turned pink with rage.

"He was not. He only borrowed a few things to take him to Paris so he could paint. Some day money would be his and then what he had borrowed would be returned. This is not to steal."

"Not to us or to Christopher," Francesco agreed. "But to The Uncle – yes. So he was told by his father and so he believes."

"But what has this to do with resting in a road?" Gussie asked.

Francesco tried to explain.

"Because of The Uncle. As he thinks Christopher was a thief, then to him it could seem there is bad in us too which must be watched, so always we must try to do well. This is why we may not know other children. They could show us something which is a Western where we could learn to do wrong."

Gussie was much quicker than Francesco when it came to picking up odds and ends of information.

"That is a box called The Telly which is in Wally's farm. I think it is like a small movie. The harm is because when such a picture is showing called a Western Wally will not go to bed."

Francesco, as so often when talking to Gussie, felt what he was trying to say slip away from him.

"But you do see, Gussie, if that is how The Uncle feels we must try very hard not to offend. We need to be much more careful than when…" he broke off, while both boys in their minds watched Togo pull their caravan along roads covered in dust while Christopher sang songs which made Olga say: "No, Christopher. Not in front of the children."

"Than when," Francesco said at last, "we had our caravan."

Inside the studio Anna was happy in a way she had not been since the earthquake. Dancing terms seemed to be the same in all languages and so was the correct positioning of the body, arms and feet. Only over one point did she and Miss de Veane differ. It was after Anna had performed a small enchaînement in the centre of the studio.

"When those shoes wear out," Miss de Veane said, "I will start you off on pointe work."

When she had said this to her other pupils there was tremendous rejoicing. For to dance on their pointes was every girl's ambitions. Anna was not pleased at all – in fact she was shocked.

"That cannot be," she told Miss de Veane. "Jardek was saying I would have my first shoes with the blocked toes when I was eleven. Now I am eight."

Miss de Veane, who, during the class, had seen in her mind's eye Anna at her next public show dancing "The Dying Swan" swallowed what she would like to have said. This was an unusual child and needed handling carefully. She collected herself inside her black dress.

"Oh well," she said to herself, "two years will soon pass."

Anna was only eight but she was sensitive and there was something in Miss de Veane's hoarse statement she did not like. So when at the end of her class she joined the boys at the door and Gussie asked how the lesson had gone she said doubtfully:

"It was good. Very good. But I do not know yet if Miss de Veane is such a teacher as Jardek would wish."

16. Uniforms

THE CHILDREN THOUGHT the school uniforms very elegant. The boys had purple blazers with the school crest on the pocket, grey socks with purple turnovers, grey shirts and purple ties and a purple school cap. Anna wore the same except she wore a grey pleated skirt and instead of a cap, since it was the autumn term, a grey felt hat with a purple ribbon round it.

Aunt Mabel had been clever. She was determined their three children should be as well turned out as all the other children, but if she bought all they needed it would use up her entire savings so she had to get Uncle Cecil to pay part of the money. Asking Cecil for money always threw her into a state so she was huffing and puffing worse than usual when she came into the lounge to speak to him.

"Ce – Ce – Cecil," she gasped. "The children start school

next week and they need uniforms."

Mabel had chosen a bad moment for Cecil was in the middle of adding a column of figures. He carefully wrote down a figure and marked where he had got to, then he put down his pen and glared at Mabel.

"The children seem adequately dressed to me. Why should they have uniforms? They can attend school in what they have."

Mabel knew it was a waste of time to say "all the other children in The Crescent wear uniform, we don't want our three to look different". Such an argument would carry no weight at all with Cecil so she had planned another.

"The boys have only cotton shirts and Anna cotton dresses. They have jerseys but since they are used to hot climates, for the autumn they should have thick coats or they will catch cold – even pneumonia."

Mabel had chosen a good argument. Cecil hated illness, and he certainly did not want talk in the neighbourhood. He opened a drawer and took out his cheque book.

"How much will overcoats cost?"

Mabel had worked out how much she needed.

"The coats should be big so they will last and they will need thick shoes. I couldn't do with less than fifty pounds."

Cecil looked as if he might have a fit.

"Fifty pounds! It's a fortune. My dear mother did not spend that much on my clothes in a year."

Mabel nodded.

"I know, dear. But fifty pounds today goes nowhere."

The children, when Mabel took them to the shops where the uniforms were sold, took their uncle's point of view.

"Why," Gussie demanded, "do we need all these clothes? We have our jerseys when like today it is cold."

"This is not what we call cold, dear," Mabel explained. "But later in the autumn and when winter comes it can be very cold and very damp and you are not used to it."

Anna suddenly remembered real cold.

"After the earthquake the cold was terrible. Even in a rug my teeth is rattling."

The assistant who was fitting out the boys pricked up her ears. These must be the children of the artist who was killed in the earthquake. The manager should know they were here. It was clear the children had not unlimited money, perhaps under such circumstances help and advice would be forthcoming, even a slight reduction.

The assistant was quite right. The manager too had read all about the Docksay children. Glowing with good feeling, he arrived at Mabel's elbow.

"Ah, Mrs Docksay, I heard you were here, and these are the three little people who escaped. Now, let me see how I can help you."

The manager did help. He seemed to know exactly how much children would grow before next summer. He knew of an exchange scheme in the school which meant outgrown uniforms could be sold. He was wonderful about overcoats, sending the assistant downstairs to bring up what he called "my special stock".

While all this was going on the children stood patiently having different garments fitted on to them. Never, even during S'William's wild outburst of extravagance in Istanbul, had they known such spending. Before the earthquake Olga would sometimes tell Christopher she must visit a bazaar because clothes were needed. But that had never meant more than a frock for Anna or some shirts or shorts for the boys. Once or twice on some celebration day Christopher would take Olga to a shop and a meal afterwards and Olga would come home giggling and wearing something very exotic, but serious top to bottom shopping they had never known. Now amazed, but stunned into patience, they found themselves with new warm underwear, school uniforms, overcoats, mackintoshes, shoes, rubber boots, new pyjamas and each a splendid dressing-gown.

"It is too much," Francesco whispered to the other two.

"Such money would pay for the most beautiful dancing classes," Anna moaned.

Gussie said nothing for he was studying the situation. In his opinion where there was so much apparently to be had without trouble there should be pickings for those who were buying. Such an arrangement was usual when much money was spent.

When all the shopping was over the manager said:

"I am sure these little people are tired. May I offer you all tea?" Then he smiled at the children and added: "With perhaps ice creams."

The invitation accepted, Gussie hung back and, when no

one was looking, took a scarf, two pairs of woollen gloves and a tie out of his pockets and laid them on the counter.

"That is the worst of Britain," he thought, "all behave too well so it is not possible to take more. It is better in Eastern countries."

Then he hurried after the others.

But Francesco had noticed Gussie was not with them. So when he caught up he whispered anxiously:

"You didn't take anything, did you?"

Gussie's face expressed shocked amazement.

"Me! Take a squeeze when the man offers ices! Such an idea!"

17. School

BEFORE SCHOOL STARTED Wally's dad had a talk with Wally. They were down by Bess's sty. Wally was cleaning out.

"When I was in that smash with me lorry," Wally's dad said, "I couldn't bring meself to talk about it, not for months I couldn't, even the insurance could only get what 'appened out of me slow like. I reckon the three Docksay kids is like that. It's not 'alf goin' to upset them if the children at the school asks too many questions."

Wally leant on his rake which he was using to clean the sty.

"I know, but what can I do about it? Maybe Francesco and me might be in the same class but the other two won't so I can't see what's 'appenin' to them."

Wally's dad wheeled his chair closer to the sty, as if he was afraid someone would hear what he said though there was only Bess there.

"I was thinkin' you might 'ave a word with the 'ead."

Wally nearly fell into the pigsty. "The 'ead! Why, I never spoken to 'im and 'ope I never will."

His dad went on calmly as if Wally had not spoken.

"I was goin' to see if your mum would go, but you know how she is, like enough just seein' the 'ead and she'll talk about you."

Wally did see. Too well he knew that his mum believed he was not properly appreciated in the school. Not promising anything, he asked:

"If I was to see the 'ead what would I say like?"

In the evenings Wally's dad sometimes went down to a pub called The George and Dragon for a pint. There the publican had a boy of Wally's age who was clever, and often the publican talked to Wally's dad about the headmaster and what an understanding man he was.

"You can do it all right, son. Just tell 'im what a state the kids get in when they remember what 'appened, 'e'll understand all right."

Wally had no idea how you saw a headmaster, but the next day he got on his bike and went to the school. He knew the headmaster would not be there, but the school keeper would and might know where he lived.

The school keeper was loading some coke into the boiler room to be ready for when central heating started. He knew Wally by sight.

" 'Ello!" he said. "Not like you to come to school when you don't 'ave to."

"It's a message I got for the 'eadmaster," Wally explained. "D'you know where 'e 'angs out?"

"You're in luck," said the school keeper, "he's inside seeing some new bookshelves what has come for the library."

The headmaster was equally surprised to see Wally.

"Hello! Wally Wall, isn't it? What can I do for you?"

Wally swallowed twice then burst without pause into his story.

"It's these Docksay kids what's coming next term. Me dad says you did oughter know what a state they gets in if anyone asks them questions. When we first sees them it was shockin' the way they cries, you see, they 'aven't nobody left not except an uncle an' an aunt, who does right by them but they don't get on like an'…"

The headmaster was a tall man. Now he laid a hand on Wally's shoulder.

"Not so fast. Let's sit down and talk this over. I think your father was quite right to tell you to see me. But what we have to think about is how best to do what needs to be done."

As a result of Wally's talk it was arranged that as soon as the children arrived for their first day at school he should take them for a guided tour round the school and the playing field. Meanwhile the headmaster would talk to the rest of the school and tell the children that the Docksay children were not to be questioned. That some day they would talk about what had happened but until then they were to be left alone.

"You try to imagine," he told the school, "what it would be like to go for a walk and come home to find your father, your mother, your brothers and sisters – all your pets and your house just disappeared. One or two of the teachers know because it could happen in the last war, but if it did, even now all these years later, it's not a thing we talk about. So you treat Francesco, Augustus and Anna just as if nothing had happened to them. I know it's hard, for we'd all like to know what it's like to be in an earthquake, but we must wait and perhaps some day they will tell us. Hands up those who understand." Every hand in the room shot up.

Francesco, Gussie and Anna liked school. It was, they found, easier than doing lessons with Olga for each worked in a separate class, whereas Olga had to try and teach all three at once though none of them was studying at the same level. The children had taken for granted Olga had taught them well, but really it was surprising for Olga's English was bad and, though she had been well educated in Turkey, she was not trained as a teacher, yet the children passed the little tests given them with, on the whole, flying colours.

The headmaster told them the results.

"You have done well, especially in arithmetic, reading and geography."

"Arithmetic we must know," Gussie explained. "When every two, three weeks it is another country and another money you must learn to add in all."

"Geography is I think easier when always you are travelling," Francesco pointed out. "But it is the Near and the Far East which is good, where a country is cold we never work."

Anna saw the caravan in her memory with Olga in her broken English reading to them from *Alice in Wonderland* or *The Wind in the Willows*.

"Because we must read Christopher buys a big box of books called *Children's Classics*. I do not remember when we could not read."

The headmaster heard a tremble in Anna's voice so he gave them all a big smile.

"But nobody taught you how to speak English."

Francesco nodded.

"Everyone said our English was bad. Christopher said it was terrible."

"So did S'William," Gussie put in, "and so does The Uncle. He is going to give us lessons and this we do not like."

"Well, I must say you can do with some lessons," the headmaster said. "Now I'll tell you what I'm going to do. I'm going to put you this term to work with people of your own ages, then later on we'll see."

The children liked school, not always the actual lesson times but the play times were fun. They soon got to know all the children in The Crescent and Francesco made friends with Jonathan and Priscilla who were in his class. But though Gussie in particular was always asking questions, neither he nor Francesco could find out how to earn fifty pence a week. They were in a junior school where the children were too young to be allowed to work. Older children, they discovered, could earn such money easily on paper rounds or helping in a shop on Saturday mornings, but for children of their age working was not permitted.

"Don't you get pocket money?" Priscilla asked Francesco. "All children do."

"How is pocket money?" Francesco asked.

All the children in the school were trying to improve Francesco's English.

"Not 'how is?' " Jonathan said. "It's 'what is?' Anyway, it's money you are given every week to spend."

Francesco was thrilled.

"Who gives such money?"

Priscilla could hear the sentence was wrong but she did not know how.

"Our father gives ours, I suppose your uncle would give yours."

Francesco knew the answer to that.

"He would not. The Aunt perhaps if she could, but I do not think she has much."

However, he passed on the news to Gussie in case he had any ideas.

"Now that we have the English lessons on Tuesdays and Thursdays could we perhaps talk about pocket money?"

The Uncle's English lessons were always conversations. He would pick out one of the children and say: "Describe what you did this morning" or "Describe what you do at recreation." Francesco always tried hard to answer correctly. Gussie wouldn't try at all and Anna was so scared of making a mistake she only spoke in a whisper. To do Uncle Cecil justice he was very patient, he merely corrected, never scolded, but there was that about his patience that made Gussie describe it as "too full a cupboard out of which any minute all would fall".

Now Gussie thought over what Francesco had said.

"It is true all but we have pocket money. Each week they give a new penny to buy a lifeboat or for a dog to lead a person who is blind. Us they do not ask because they know we have nothing."

"Some pay for school meals," said Anna. "For this they have much money to pay, in one week more I think than the whole dancing class."

Gussie gave Anna a dirty look.

"If you think I am going to starve for your lessons you are wrong."

"Nor will The Uncle pay for the school dinners," Francesco pointed out. "He says sandwiches is better. And I think so too, it is terrible what they had yesterday, that thing called a cottage pie and prunes covered in custard."

"Always the sandwiches are not good," Francesco agreed, "but often they are and The Aunt cuts pages out of papers to find new things to put in them which taste good to eat."

"We must try the pocket money," Gussie said. "Today is the lesson, let us agree the first one he asks a question of talks of pocket money."

"Oh no," Anna pleaded, "not if it's me. I will do it wrong."

Gussie looked at Francesco.

"So she would. The first of us two. It is agreed."

"I suppose so," Francesco said gloomily.

That evening when the children came into the lounge and sat on the sofa it so happened The Uncle started with Gussie.

"Describe to me, Augustus, your school library."

"It is a room by itself and each day two boys is..."

"Are," said The Uncle.

"Two boys are looking after it. We go at the dinner break and change a book."

"The books are free?" The Uncle asked. This was of course Gussie's chance.

"Yes, otherwise all in the school..."

"Everyone in the school," The Uncle corrected.

"Would get books except us, we would have no books because we have no pocket money."

Uncle Cecil was silent for a moment. The truth was he had forgotten pocket money. But when he had been a boy there had been some. A penny for church on Sunday. Three pennies towards school charities and two pennies for himself. Christopher, when he was old enough for school, had only pretended to put a penny in the bag on Sundays and had never given a farthing to school charities, but had secretly spent his whole sixpence on painting materials. Uncle Cecil turned to Francesco.

"If you had pocket money, Francesco, on what would you spend it?"

Francesco told the other two afterwards he so longed to say "on dancing lessons for Anna" that he nearly did. Then, just in time, he stopped himself. Trying desperately to speak good English so as not to offend he said:

"As the other children do. There is – I mean are – many school charities to which all give. This week I think we will buy a lifeboat."

Uncle Cecil of course understood that money today would not go as far as it had when he was at school, so, feeling very generous, he decided to double what he had received.

"Every week," he said in a grand voice, "each of you will receive five pence."

18. Francesco's Turn

OF COURSE THE children could not use their pocket money either for school charities or for themselves. Every penny would be needed for Anna's dancing classes, and obviously fifteen pence a week would be a great help. All the same, it still left a lot to be found and not one word from S'William. Not knowing that Sir William was capable of leaving an unposted letter in his pocket for six weeks the children worried, for of course they knew how easy it was to be well and happy in the morning and to have vanished for ever by the evening.

One night in bed Francesco said to Gussie:

"No one has said something has happened in Alaska. I asked Wally to ask his dad, for he reads two papers but he says there has been nothing in the news."

There was now only one week's money left to pay for

Anna's classes. Gussie found it hard never to have sweets when others did.

"I was thinking that our five pence should be saved for a week when we have earned nothing. Then some weeks we might not need it."

Francesco sat up in bed.

"I do not know yet of a week when we can earn anything. Not unless Wally hears of something. He is trying hard."

"What I think," said Gussie, "is that we should take turns – you the first week, me the second. Then it could be sometimes we have our pocket money to ourselves. Not perhaps Anna as she is causing us to work but you and me."

Francesco was suspicious.

"Have you a plan?"

Gussie sounded cautious.

"No. But – I have ideas."

Francesco leant over towards Gussie's bed.

"Do tell me before you do anything. There is not the same rules in Britain as there was in the places we knew. Then to beg was honourable and to take a squeeze from the shopping correct, but here it is not so."

Gussie smiled in the darkness.

"Do you think I don't know! You get the fifty pence your way and I will find a way to get mine."

Francesco found it hard to sleep that night. If only he knew what Gussie was planning. But since they had been going to school Gussie had gone his own way and made his own friends and Francesco was not sure they were good friends for him. Wally had put this idea into his head.

"Young Gus has picked up with The Gang."

Francesco's English was improving rapidly. So he swallowed back "How is a gang?" and instead asked what it was.

"It's them from the new block of flats. They're what's called re'oused from farther off an' by what's said they're a rough lot. You know, breaking public telephones and that for fun."

"Why is that fun?" Francesco had asked.

Wally couldn't explain exactly.

"Just for somethin' to do, I reckon, but young Gus did ought to watch out, for the coppers 'ave their eyes on a lot like that."

Now, tossing in bed, Francesco thought of what Gussie had said. "You get fifty pence your way and I'll find a way to get mine." But what would be Gussie's way? Oh dear, if only S'William were back. Then he had an idea and it was this which sent him to sleep. Tomorrow he would write to S'William so at least he would get a letter the moment he returned to England.

The one person who never appeared to worry at all where fifty pence was coming from was Anna. It was true that she spent most of her free time thinking about her dancing, and working at exercises in her bedroom, but the truth was that she had a secret worry of her own as well. She was almost sure that Miss de Veane, though she had not said so, was planning that she dance in her public performance at Christmas. After a lesson she would say:

"Before you go, Anna, do this enchaînement for me. Wait, I will put some music on the gramophone."

And then Anna was given a series of steps which she could guess was part of a dance. It was lovely to do and made her feel much more that she was really dancing than exercises did, but she knew it was wrong. Jardek would never have allowed it. But what was she to do if Miss de Veane ordered her to dance? She had learnt a lot since she came to Fyton, and one of the things she had learnt was that until S'William returned and the picture could be sold she must learn from Miss de Veane, for she was the only teacher there was. There would be other teachers in London but London was many miles away and she had no means of getting there.

It was natural now for Anna to go to Francesco when she had a problem, so she went to him about her dancing lessons. He should know what she most feared. In the last two weeks only Francesco had taken Anna to her class. Gussie, on the days when they did not learn English with Uncle Cecil, had taken to slipping off after school with his friends. This Wednesday, on the way home from her dancing class, Anna said to Francesco:

"That was the last of our money. Will you have another fifty pence for next week?"

Francesco had no idea where his fifty pence was coming from but he did not want to worry Anna.

"It will be ready for next Wednesday."

Anna tried to explain what was troubling her.

"I think perhaps if Miss de Veane knew we have no money she would teach me for nothing."

Francesco could have jumped like a kangaroo. For nothing! No more worrying where fifty pence was coming from! However, he spoke cautiously for there was no knowing what Anna felt.

"Why should she?"

Anna looked up at him and her eyes were full of anxiety.

"I think perhaps Jardek taught better even than we knew. At Christmas Miss de Veane gives a great performance in a concert hall, it is for some charity. At such a concert all she has taught, dance – girls like Doreen. I think she would wish me to dance so all would think it was not Jardek who had taught me but that she had. So more pupils come."

Francesco was shocked.

"But you are only eight. Jardek would never permit this."

"I am nearly nine," Anna reminded him. "And Jardek is no longer here."

This was so miserable a thought that they walked in silence for a moment, almost on tiptoe so that what little they still had of Jardek would not be disturbed. Then Francesco asked:

"Has she said she wishes you to dance?"

Anna shook her head.

"No. But I feel she is planning. If once she knew it was hard to find the money I think she would offer lessons, but in return I must do in all things as she says."

Francesco was no stranger to such arrangements. Often when they had travelled by caravan they had met children who, in exchange for a bed, clothes and food were somebody's little slave. Sometimes it had worked well but often it had not. The thought of selling Anna into such a life appalled him.

"Miss de Veane must never, never know it is hard to find the money. You must let her think if each lesson is costing a whole pound we do not care. There is always plenty of money."

Anna took Francesco's hand and rubbed her face against his sleeve.

"When you talk so it is as if Olga is back."

She could not have said anything nicer.

But still Francesco had not got fifty pence, not if he used all their pocket money, and the next class was one week away.

19. Saturday at Wally's

WHAT WITH THE days growing shorter and school taking up much time, and Uncle Cecil's English lessons, the children were seeing very little of Wally's family. They did of course see Wally at school but only Francesco saw him to talk to because they were in the same class. There was never a chance that they would walk to school together because Wally rode there on his bicycle, whereas the children got there by walking up The Crescent.

"I don't like it," Wally's mum would grumble. "They was sent to us like and I'd be much happier in meself if I could keep an eye on them like."

Wally's dad agreed with her for he knew he would be much happier too, but it was hard to figure a way of seeing the children. Then that very Saturday morning, when Wally was looking after the stall, his mum had a piece of luck. She was in the supermarket, her trolley piled high with the week's shopping. At the place where you pay there was a woman stacking her shopping on the counter.

"Nice weather for the time of year," the assistant said to her.

The woman, sorting out what she had bought, seemed overcome by this casual remark. She puffed and gasped and dropped a packet of breakfast cereal and half a pound of tea on to the floor. Wally's mum stopped to help her pick the packets up and as she did so something about the woman struck her. What was it the children had said? "The Aunt seems only held together by her apron." Well, she hadn't an apron on now but she did look as if she was held together by her coat buttons. The children had also said she had hair which always looked as if it might tumble down. Well, certainly this woman had hair like it was straggling out from under her shapeless felt hat. Then Gussie had said The Aunt was like a mouse – afraid to move unless a cat was coming. "Poor lady," Wally's mum thought, "if ever anyone looked scared of a cat, she does."

The woman panted out a weak "thank you" and went back to sorting out her shopping, and it was then Wally's mum decided to take a chance. "Seemed like me duty really," she told Wally's dad when she got home.

"S'cuse me," she said, "but would you be Mrs Docksay?"

The assistant and Wally's mum put out hands to make sure Aunt Mabel did not drop anything more on to the floor. Then Aunt Mabel squeaked:

"Yes."

"Perhaps then you'd 'ave a cuppa tea with me," said Wally's mum. "You see, I know the children, in fact your Francesco is in a class with my Wally at the school and they're pals like."

Presently in a nearby tea shop Wally's mum and Mabel were drinking tea.

"I know 'ow you're placed, dear," Wally's mum said. "Your ole man's not the only one that likes to keep 'imself to 'imself but the children won't come to any 'arm along of us. I was thinkin' it would be nice if you could let them come along of a Saturday afternoon, maybe Sundays too."

With a tremendous effort Mabel managed to explain Cecil's outlook.

"You see, he was brought up to think the children's father took what did not belong to him: of course he didn't really, he only borrowed, at least that's what he thought, but you know how it is, what you are told as a fact sticks. Anyway, he won't let our children mix with other children in case they should be a bad influence. He doesn't want them to see television."

Wally's mum laughed.

"What I always say is what the eye doesn't see the 'eart doesn't grieve after. Course the telly's on in our 'ouse on a Saturday – catch my ole man missing 'is football – but what's the 'arm in a game of football? Nor Wally wouldn't miss it either come to that."

Mabel had brightened up but she still spoke in jerks.

"I'm sure football would be all right. As a matter of fact, I have worried rather about Saturdays and Sundays now the days are drawing in. You see, Mr Docksay likes the house quiet but it's difficult for the children to be quiet when they've nothing much to do and nowhere to go."

Wally's mum decided to get the matter fixed. She got up.

"Well, I got to go but I'll expect the children later. Can they stop to tea?"

Mabel picked her shopping bag up off the floor.

"Well, they must be home by half past five at the latest or my husband might notice they were out." She flushed. "You see, I shall let him think they're having tea in the kitchen."

The children were charmed when before lunch their aunt told them they could visit Mrs Wall.

"Such a nice woman," she said, "but you must slip out quietly and be back sharp at five-thirty."

"They've got a farm," Anna told her. "Hens and a pig called Bessie. It's lovely, they're not too tidy and everyone is pleased you are there, almost like..." She broke off.

Francesco helped Anna out.

"She's right. In a sort of British way it is perhaps as little like it was at Jardek and Babka's."

When Wally's mum saw the children she held out her arms and gave them one gigantic hug.

"I 'ope you 'ad a word with the 'ens and Bess on the way up. You won't get out again for the football's started and Mr Wall thinks, like 'e does most weeks, 'e's goin' to win the pools." She looked questioningly at Anna. "You keen on football, dearie?"

"We've none of us seen it except when we play at school,"
Gussie explained.

"You go and look too, dear," Wally's mum told Anna, "but
if you don't fancy it, which I don't meself, you come in the
kitchen and we'll trim up the cake what I've made for tea."

Anna watched the TV for a little while but she did not
understand football, nor Wally and his dad's explanations,
which the boys seemed to find absorbing, so she slipped away
to the kitchen.

"And I bet not one of 'em knew you'd gone," said Mrs
Wall.

"No, none of them."

Mrs Wall gave Anna some cherries and nuts and told her
to trim the cake.

"Well," she asked, "how's the dancin' goin?"

Anna trusted Wally's mum.

"Sort of well. I mean Miss de Veane teaches well, I think,
almost as if it is Jardek, but I do not know how she is
thinking."

"How d'you mean, dear?"

Anna made a pattern of nuts and cherries.

"At Christmas she is giving a show…"

"Oh, you mean her concert. Does one every year for a
charity. That Doreen dances a special piece on her own, so I
'ear."

Anna sounded determined.

"Jardek would never allow this. I do not know but I think
Miss de Veane wishes me to dance on the pointes."

Anna sounded so appalled that Wally's mum tried to feel shocked too. Only she had no idea what Anna was talking about.

"Oh, my word!"

"Imagine! And I am not yet nine and Jardek said not until I was eleven."

"But unless I got thin's wrong you can't learn with this Miss de Veane much longer. You only 'ad the money for five lessons, didn't you?"

Anna gazed at Wally's mum with horror-struck eyes.

"But I must learn with her, that is until S'William is back and we can sell our picture. You see, in this place there is no one else."

"But isn't it fifty pence a week, dear? Where's that coming from?"

Over Anna's face there seemed to fall a curtain. Wally's mum could not know that Anna was hearing Jardek say in Polish and broken English: "A dancer must live for nothing but dancing. Anything that comes between a dancer and dancing must be absolutely forgotten." So she must not think where fifty pence was coming from: it would appear. She put a final cherry on the cake. Her voice was calm and confident.

"This week Francesco pays. Next week it will be Gussie."

The football had been a great success. In fact Wally, his dad and the boys could not leave it, so they had their tea sitting round the box.

"I don't want to rush anybody," Wally's mum said, "but I did promise your auntie you'd be home by five-thirty sharp."

Looking at the boys' faces as she brought round the food Wally's mum decided Francesco did not look as well as she would like, he had those same dark smudges under his eyes all three children had had when they arrived. And he didn't eat nearly as well as Gussie, who wolfed three sandwiches with pickled onions before he started on the cake.

After tea when the children had left and Wally and she had gone out to shut up the hens, Wally's mum said:

"I don't think young Francesco's lookin' good. No trouble at the school, is there?"

Wally shoved the last of the hens into the run.

"No, not there, 'e does well at school. I think it's money, 'e's always on at me to find a way 'e can earn."

"And 'ave you 'elped 'im?"

"I don't see a way," Wally confessed. "You see, 'e's only ten. And there's no gardenin' this late in the year."

Mrs Wall fastened the door of the chicken run.

"Tell you what, when the kids come along tomorrow get out of 'im what 'is trouble is. Shouldn't wonder if it's Anna's dancin' lesson. But whatever it is let 'im talk it over with you. For troubles shared is troubles 'alved, and 'e is your friend."

20. The Sacrifice

AS SUNDAY TURNED out it was easy for Wally to get Francesco alone, for Wally's dad decided to give Gussie's hair another cut.

"Your uncle will be creatin' about it again any day now," he said. "Give us the basin and a towel, Wally."

"But if we wait until he says something," Gussie argued, "he'll give me twenty-five pence like he did before. And we need it extra bad because we spent the end of the suitcase money on Anna's last lesson."

"Because I let you take your uncle's money the once it don't mean I'm makin' a habit of it. Now sit down and don't wriggle or I'll 'ave a ear off of you."

"You come into the kitchen, Anna," said Wally's mum. "And 'ave a look at what I've got. Next week I gets me Christmas puddin's started. You ever ate a Christmas puddin'?"

Anna never had nor did she know what it was. Unwillingly she pulled her mind to look at past Christmases. Christopher had always driven the caravan to Jardek and Babka's little house for Christmas. Anna could almost see them arrive, perhaps as late as the morning on Christmas Eve, with bells tied on Togo's harness and red ribbons plaited in his tail.

"I do not know a Christmas pudding but always there was cakes, piles of cakes. Babka made them."

Wally's mum saw it was hurting Anna to talk about Christmas. For everybody who has someone to miss, Christmas is the worst time for missing them. But Christmas would come just the same, so it was best the children should face it. She had an easy chair by the window. Now she sat down in it and held out her arms to Anna.

"Come and sit on my knee and tell me all about your Christmas, then I'll tell you how we keep it 'ere."

Anna climbed on to Wally's mum's cosy lap.

"Christmas Eve was as Babka and Jardek knew it when they were little and lived in Poland. Christmas Day was for Christopher but not very much except for presents, for he said there should be a turkey but often it was not possible to buy one."

"What happened on Christmas Eve?" Wally's mum asked.

Anna tried to remember it all.

"You eat fish. That is because it is a fast. When Jardek and Babka were little always after the fish were many, many more dishes but of course we did not eat like that. The first thing for the Christmas Eve dinner was when we covered the table with straw."

"Straw!" said Wally's mum. "What would you put straw on the table for?"

Anna screwed up her face trying to remember.

"It was sort of holy straw. After we had eaten Babka took it out to Togo. She did not let Christopher see because he would laugh and it is not good to laugh at what is holy, but Babka told us such straw, if eaten by Togo, would keep him in health for a whole year."

"Well, that was nice," said Wally's mum. "Maybe I better put some straw on the table for Bess and the hens. Do you put the cloth over it?"

Anna was remembering better.

"Oh yes, the best tablecloth. Then when all were sitting Babka brought in the soup. This was always made with almonds and was beautiful. Then came the fish with so many different sauces you could not count."

"My goodness!" said Wally's mum. "I'm glad we don't do that here on Christmas Eve or I'd never get up of a Christmas morning."

Anna was almost tasting things now.

"Then comes the cakes. The best is called pirogi. This looks like a little loaf of bread but inside it is all almond paste and poppy seeds. Always Gussie had to be stopped eating them or he was sick. As well there are other cakes and fruits dried in sugar."

Wally's mum was getting confused.

"But what did you do on Christmas Day? Didn't you hang up a sock or stocking?"

Anna shook her head.

"None of us had socks or stockings till S'William bought them. And why should we hang them up?"

"Children get presents in them."

Anna leant back against Wally's mum's warm shoulder.

"But we did have presents – things Christopher had bought, but best was the outside for on each one he painted a picture, sometimes…"

Anna's voice had faded away. It was too much. Those parcels of Christopher's, so beautiful and often so funny. Never, never to have one again.

Wally's mum lifted Anna off her knee.

"You come over here and I'll show you what I put in me Christmas puddin'."

Wally was not used to making excuses to talk to people. Whatever he had to say just came straight out. Still, his mum had said he was to let Francesco talk so he knew he had to do it.

"I got to oil me bike," he said to Francesco. "You comin'?"

The bike was kept in a lean-to which was just a piece of corrugated iron leaning against the hen house. Because Wally's bike was there, and an upturned wooden box made a kind of work bench, it had always seemed to Francesco and Gussie a most desirable place to own.

"All his very own," Gussie had said enviously, "and to have a bicycle too!"

Wally started to oil his bicycle. He hoped his mum was right, she usually was, but it seemed to him like poking his nose in where it was not wanted to ask Francesco questions. At last he said:

"What's 'appenin'? I mean about fifty pence for Anna's next lesson? Can you do it out of that pocket money?"

Francesco did not answer at once, so Wally looked up at him and saw he was swallowing as if he was trying not to cry. At last Francesco said in a voice which sounded not as if he was talking to Wally, but to anyone anywhere:

"Always things was easy. Christopher thought of nothing but pictures, but if something had to be decided then Olga took away his canvas and perhaps his paints and he could not have them back until the decision is made. Now there is nobody, only me, and I do not know what is right to do. We could perhaps with the pocket money find enough for one more lesson but one is not enough, it is each week this great sum we must have. This Wednesday I should pay and the next Gussie, but for this Wednesday, except the pocket money, I have nothing – nothing at all."

Wally tried to find the right words to ask a question.

"Will it be so shockin' bad if Anna doesn't 'ave a lesson until S'William comes 'ome and you can sell your picture?"

Francesco choked back a sob.

"But will he come? He gave us his address and I have written with the right stamp."

"What did you say?"

"I didn't know how to spell S'William so I just said 'Please to come and see us, it is urgent that we sell our picture with many felicitations love Francesco.' "

"I wouldn't worry, 'e'll come."

"But suppose he never does? You do not understand, Wally. Anna must learn, for her not to learn is a very, very bad sin."

Wally wiped down his bicycle with a rag.

"What I don't see is why you 'ave to get in a state about it. It isn't as though you could do anythin'."

Francesco looked at Wally and there were tears in his eyes.

"I had never known how it is to be the eldest. All is now in my care. There is nobody else. Nobody at all."

"Come on," said Wally, "race you to the 'ouse, we've 'ot toast with relish for tea."

The next morning in the playground at break Wally drew Francesco into a corner. There he took an envelope out of his pocket, and in it was £1.50.

"Go on, take it," he said to Francesco. "It's for you. It'll pay for three lessons and with the three Gussie's payin' for that's six weeks, and I reckon S'William'll be 'ome by then."

Francesco had turned first white, and then red.

"One pound and fifty pence! Where did you get such money?"

Wally made a face at him.

"No need to look suspicious. I come by it honest." He struggled to sound casual. "If you want to know, I sold me bike."

Francesco was horrified. The bike, though old and clattery, was, as all knew, the pride of Wally's life.

"I can't take it. You must get the bicycle back."

"There's gratitude for you," Wally jeered. " 'Get it back,' he says, I know it wasn't up to much but it was dirt cheap at one fifty and 'im that bought it knows it. 'E won't give it to me back, 'e's been on at me for months to sell it to 'im."

Francesco looked at the money as if it was the crock of gold from under the rainbow.

"It is too much," he whispered, "but some day, perhaps when we sell the picture, there will be a new bicycle for you."

Wally did not believe any picture was worth the price of a bicycle but he didn't say so. Instead he changed the subject.

"Now mind you, nobody isn't to know 'ow you got the money. Nobody – not Gussie, not Anna – nobody. I just might tell me mum, for she'll see it's missin', but that's all."

Francesco, moved almost past speech by Wally's generosity, could only nod.

"I promise," he whispered.

It was on the way home from school that Gussie learnt that Francesco had raised his share of the money for Anna's lessons. Anna brought the subject up.

"I wish S'William would come home. I need a dress, Miss de Veane calls it a tunic, for dancing. School clothes is not right and I have no others."

Gussie looked at Anna rather as a mother bird must sometimes look at its ever-hungry young.

"A tunic! Here's me and Francesco not knowing how to earn fifty pence each week, it's a lot of money, and now you ask for tunics!"

"Don't worry, Anna," said Francesco. "I have enough for three lessons without using our pocket money, perhaps that could buy a tunic. Also, I think The Aunt would help."

Gussie had not got over his habit of sitting or lying down when he felt like it. Now he sat down on the pavement.

"What! You have money for three lessons! How?"

"I have it and that is enough," said Francesco. Then he opened his hand and showed them Wally's coins.

Gussie was furious. He knew in the most secret place in his soul that he was by far the smartest of the family. He had been convinced that he alone was within smelling distance of a way to raise money, and here was Francesco, so slow and so tiresome about what was right and what was wrong, with one pound fifty. In that second he knew what he must try to do. He had hesitated before but now it was certain. He got to his feet and, looking terribly proud, faced Anna and Francesco. He thumped his chest "Me, Gussie, will have enough for four lessons."

21. The Gang

ALTHOUGH GUSSIE HAD spoken in a bragging way about getting two pounds by Wednesday week he knew inside himself that, though he had a plan, he had very little idea how to carry it out.

At school there was quite a large group of children who lived in a block of flats just outside Fyton. These children belonged to families who had been rehoused from slum clearance areas from other parts of the country. Many of these families had settled down well and had friends all over Fyton, but there was a small element of what the police called "troublemakers". Many of this group had younger brothers and some of these were in Gussie's class. They were known as The Gang and Gussie admired them enormously.

To admire people does not mean they want to become your friends so, try as Gussie would, he had remained a kind of admiring hanger-on. What drew him to The Gang was not just that they appeared to share exciting secrets but that somehow all of them seemed to have money. It had been his ambition to work his way in and then to startle Francesco by throwing down a fifty-pence piece when his turn came, saying casually: "There is plenty more where that came from."

Now the unthinkable had happened. It was Francesco who had the money while he, clever Gussie, looked as if it was he who would have to use the pocket money when his turn came.

He was faced with having to get fifty pence. Gussie considered The Gang carefully. He had not done this before, when he felt the day when he would actually have to pay for a dancing class was miles away, and indeed might never come for surely S'William would be home soon. The Gang was mostly made up of boys of nine and ten but the leaders were big boys of eleven who would soon be moving on to a senior school. These big boys would sometimes call the younger boys into a corner of the school yard and either tell them something or give them something. Gussie, on the outskirts of the group, had never known what went on, but he had succeeded in looking as if he did and that was all that then had mattered to him. But now he had to find out what went on for he was sure that whatever it was that happened had to do with money.

Gussie was popular with his class for he did not mind what he said, and often just in the way he said things the children found him funny, but he had not yet made an especial friend unless he could count Tom. Tom was a member of The Gang. He was a pale boy with hair so fair it was almost white, pale pinkish eyes behind glasses with thick lenses and a look as if he never got enough to eat. This last was not true for Gussie knew what food Tom brought for his lunch and it was enough for six of him. Gussie had sort of made friends with Tom because Tom was very fond of his curry, something his mother never put in his sandwiches, but which Aunt Mabel, forever studying, had learnt to make for the children. So Gussie now and then swapped a curry sandwich with Tom, not because he liked Tom's meat sandwiches but because he was good-natured.

The day after Francesco's revelation that he had £1.50, there were curry sandwiches in the children's lunch boxes so in break time Gussie went straight to Tom.

"We've got curry today. It will be curried chicken for we had chicken on Sunday. Want to swap?"

Tom did, so a pact was made that the swap would take place in the classroom at dinner time. But when dinner time came Tom dashed over to Gussie.

"Come on. Swap quick. There's a buzz. I'm wanted in the playground."

Gussie was not having that.

"All right. I'll come with you. We'll swap outside."

The Gang meeting was the same as usual. Those close to the leaders, which included Tom, clustered together in a corner. The outer ring, which included Gussie, saw and heard nothing. But this time Gussie made sure he did not lose sight of Tom. The moment The Gang broke up he had him by the arm.

"Come on and swap. I'm starving."

Tom and Gussie sat together on one of the big coal bunkers which were near the school keeper's house. Gussie proudly laid out three beautiful curried chicken sandwiches; his mouth watered as he looked at them. Tom pushed forward three great sandwiches of coarsely cut bread, one full of beef, one of pork and one of cheese. Gussie shuddered but he took them.

"Bit of all right your auntie's sandwiches," said Tom with his mouth full. "but it's odd you don't 'ave school dinners like the others from The Crescent."

Gussie groaned.

"The food we eat at The Uncle's is terrible. That cabbage! But school meals – no, that is not to be endured. The Aunt knows this. What were you saying to The Gang?"

Tom took another enormous mouthful of sandwich.

"Nothin' you want. You see, you got no money. We was given some thin's to sell like."

Tom looked around to see nobody was watching them.

"Mostly thin's the girls like." He whipped a scarf out of a pocket. It was bright green with squirly patterns on it. "This is just one, we got 'em in all colours."

"Then you sell them?"

"That's the ticket. Mind you, it's fair do's for they're cheaper than they are in the shops."

"But where do you get them from?"

Tom looked vague.

"That's up to the leaders. Maybe they're what's called rejects from a factory."

"Then if you sell them do you get the money for them?" Gussie asked.

"That's the ticket. They cost fifty pence and if I sells one I get ten for meself. It soon mounts up."

Gussie could imagine that it did. He could imagine too how many such scarves Mrs Wall might sell on her stall. Why, he only had to sell five and he would have fifty pence.

"I would like to sell such scarves," he said.

Tom looked doubtful.

"Who to?"

"Well there is The Aunt, she will buy one, and there is someone else I know who might buy many."

Tom finished the last curry sandwich and started off on a beef one.

"I can't get you scarves nor nothin' else to sell jus' like that. I got to tell somebody you're willin', then, if he says 'yes' you swears a vow to obey the leaders even in the face of death. Then they cuts your arm so your blood mixes with their blood. Then they sets you a task and if you do that OK you're in."

Gussie was enthralled. Just for the right to sell a few scarves it sounded wildly exciting.

"When can you tell the somebody? Because I want to have fifty pence earned by the Wednesday after this one."

Tom went on chewing.

"That should be easy. But mind you're sure you want to do it, for if you wasn't to keep the vow 'avin' made it they'd kill you, straight they would."

Gussie was carried away by the whole idea of joining The Gang. He thumped his chest.

"You do not worry. Me, Gussie, when I swear a vow I swear it. The vow is kept."

22. The Letter

THE NEXT DAY Sir William's letter came. Aunt Mabel had it in her apron pocket. She gave it to Francesco when he came in from school.

"It's from Sir William, it's got his name on the back. Take it upstairs to read. I don't know why but just hearing his name upsets your uncle. Luckily he hasn't seen it."

The three children went into the boys' bedroom. It was of course the letter Sir William had written on the aeroplane and forgotten to post for six weeks. Francesco read it out loud to the other two. The beginning part saying he would not be away long and that when he came back he would ask permission from their uncle to take them out was received with interruptions from Gussie.

"How does he mean 'not away long'? Already it is months."

"I do not believe he is ever coming back."

"Why does he say nothing of our picture?"

The last part made Anna turn quite white with excitement.

*If, Anna, you are not fixed up with a suitable dancing
teacher I hear very good accounts of a Madame Scarletti.
I looked her up in the telephone book. She has a studio
at 45 Bemberton Street, Chelsea, London. I gather she
is very old but still one of the best teachers in the world.*

"Madame Scarletti!" Anna whispered, as if they were magic
words. "One of the best teachers in the world."

Gussie, who had been lying on the floor, jumped to his
feet.

"You be quiet," he shouted at Anna. "You cannot go to
Madame Scarletti until the picture is sold. And now I do not
think it ever will be sold because I think S'William has stolen
it. Always you want something. First it is private lessons. Then
it is a tunic. Now it is a Madame who lives in London where
you cannot get..."

Gussie might have shouted more for he was very angry,
but the door opened and Aunt Mabel, looking worried,
peered in.

"Oh, don't quarrel, dears. We could hear you in the
lounge with the door shut, and you know how your uncle
dislikes noise."

Gussie was so angry with Anna that he might have gone
on shouting, only Anna and her one-track mind prevented

him. S'William's letter and Gussie's shouts had reminded her of her tunic.

"Aunt Mabel, I need a tunic for dancing." At the mention of dancing Aunt Mabel's head looked like disappearing, for, though she knew that somehow Anna was learning, she did not admit even to herself that she knew that she knew. But Anna was too quick for her. She darted to the door and gripped Aunt Mabel by a sleeve of her jersey. "It is simple to make and the material need cost very little, or we have our pocket money which could buy it." Gussie groaned. "But now I must have a tunic because…"

This time it was Francesco who interrupted for he felt sure Anna, in her excited state, was going to mention Madame Scarletti.

"She does need a tunic," he said quietly. "Perhaps she could explain after tea before the English lesson."

Aunt Mabel nodded.

"A tunic. You shall have it, Anna." Then she was gone.

This dramatic disappearance made Gussie forget he was angry.

"You see," he said. "Is she not exactly as a mouse who has seen a cat?"

Francesco opened the door of the cupboard in which they kept Sir William's address under the lining paper and put Sir William's letter beside it.

"Now we must get ready for tea and the English lesson," he said. Then he added in what he was afraid was becoming a special older brother voice: "Now don't forget, either of you, no one – no one at all must know what is in that letter. If it is necessary some day Anna may have to go to London but no one, not even Wally's mum would agree to that if they knew."

The children always had their tea in the kitchen. This meant Cecil had his tea in peace alone with Mabel and the children, provided they kept their voices down, could talk as much as they liked. As well, in their opinion, they had much better food all of a savoury nature, whereas in the lounge there was thin bread and butter and a horrible cake full of seeds. That day of course they talked about the letter. Francesco for once did most of the talking.

"It does not matter yet, Anna, how well this Madame Scarletti teaches. You cannot see her because you cannot go to London. But when there is holidays perhaps a way can be found. Now you have Miss de Veane and that is enough."

"I should think it was," Gussie growled. "At fifty pence each week. And if you saw this Madame Scarletti I should think she would cost five pounds each week."

Anna looked trustingly at Francesco.

"It is knowing she is there that is mattering. I do not know how Miss de Veane thinks, if she thinks wrong I now know where else I can learn."

Gussie leant across the table.

"If The Uncle had heard how you spoke that English, Anna, I think he would have a fit and perhaps die, which, though a good idea, would mean you couldn't learn at all for we would have no home."

Aunt Mabel asked no questions about the tunic. She accepted the pattern Anna gave her and said when ready she would put it on her bed.

"Now be careful in your English lesson," she warned all three children. "Your uncle is still a little upset by the noise you made upstairs."

As it turned out, the noise Gussie had made had good results. As it was getting towards Christmas Uncle Cecil was getting busier, for all the charities he worked for sold things like Christmas cards at Christmas and that meant a lot of work for the Treasurer. He had come in tired that afternoon with a bit of a headache and Gussie's shouts from upstairs had been the last straw. Over tea he had thought seriously about the children's English. There was no doubt about it – all three had greatly improved. His lessons consisting of conversation on intelligent subjects, such as "Tell me what impressed you most in Istanbul?" or "What do you know about the Magna Carta?" were succeeding. Gussie's replies to any question were painfully frivolous, but on the other hand his English was quite fluent. Perhaps the day had come when the lessons could be given up and he could leave the children's English to their teachers at school, so when the children were sitting in a row on the velvet sofa he said:

"Francesco, do you think your English has improved?"

Francesco felt worried. If he said it had The Uncle might be angry and say it was still terrible. But if he said it was still bad he might think they had not worked during his lessons.

"I hope it is better." Francesco spoke with caution. "It

should be with the conversation lessons as well as school."

"And what do you think, Augustus?"

"I think we speak so good – I mean well – that soon it is us who will be giving English lessons."

"And what do you think, Anna?"

Anna was so scared during English lessons she always spoke in a whisper.

"I know I speak better, a teacher at school told me so."

Cecil could hardly resist letting out a sigh of relief. He had found the English lessons a great trial and he was thankful from the bottom of his heart that no one had made him a schoolteacher. He was thankful too that he and Mabel had no children, but he was still furious at the bad luck which had landed his robbing wastrel of a brother's children on him.

"I agree with your teacher, Anna," he said, "so I have decided this will be your last lesson. Instead ask your teachers for books from the school library. There is nothing like reading a good book to improve your English. Now go to your rooms and start your homework. And go quietly."

All the children crept up to the boys' room. Then, when the door was shut, stuffing their handkerchiefs in their mouths to shut out the sound of laughter, they rolled on the floor, occasionally snatching out their handkerchiefs to say "A good book!" "The last lesson!" They did not know it but it was the first time they had laughed like that since the earthquake and they didn't even notice there was no Christopher to say, "Shut up, you kids, I will have hush."

23. Wilf

Tom, though he preferred to remain in the background, did speak to The Gang's leader about Gussie. This was a big boy called Wilf. He had dirty fair hair which nearly reached his shoulders and he wore a jersey with a skull and crossbones woven on to it. All the smaller boys were scared of him, for if they displeased him he didn't wait to hear an excuse but out came his fists and he was a good boxer.

There was never a teachers' meeting but Wilf's name came up, for all the teachers considered him a menace and longed for the day when he would move on to another school.

"I'm sure he's a bad influence," the headmaster was always saying. "And I shouldn't wonder if he was a thief. Any day I'm expecting to hear he's in juvenile court."

Tom had sold his scarf, so it was easy for him to speak to

Wilf for he had to see him to give him the money. Passing over the money was always done when nobody was about, but Wilf had several tough friends who watched out for him to see if the coast was clear. The Gang had a pass sign of thumping one fist on the other. Tom gave this sign and was allowed into the senior classroom where Wilf was sitting alone at his desk. Tom came up to the desk and laid down forty pence.

"Where'd you sell it?" Wilf asked.

"One of the girls bought it for her mum's birthday."

"Where did you say you'd got it?"

"Sellin' it cheap, I said, for a friend what's got a shop London way."

Wilf nodded both to show he approved and to dismiss Tom, but Tom did not move so Wilf asked:

"Well? What is it?"

"There's a boy in my class called Gussie Docksay. 'E wants to join."

" 'Ow does 'e know there's anythin' to join?"

" 'E's one of the kids what 'angs around when we meet in the playground."

"Gussie Docksay. Isn't 'e one of the kids what was in that earthquake?"

"That's right."

There was a cunning smile on Wilf's face.

"Live up The Crescent?"

"That's right."

Wilf came to a decision.

"Go and find 'im, I'll see 'im now."

Gussie had no idea that Wilf was to be feared. He knew him by sight of course, as did everybody in the school, but he had never spoken to him. So when Tom took him to the classroom door and told him to go in he went in afraid of nothing except that Wilf might refuse to let him join The Gang.

Wilf looked at Gussie and rather liked what he saw. Gussie was small for his age but he looked tough, intelligent and noticeably unafraid.

"Why do you want to join?" Wilf asked.

"Money," Gussie explained. "It's not for me but I have a sister who must learn to dance. She has private lessons, each one costs fifty pence. This I must earn for I pay every other week. My brother Francesco has three weeks' money but I have none and this I do not like."

Wilf had not listened to half of this.

"Now an' then I gets thin's to sell. Where they comes from is none of your business, but if you was caught sellin' and asked where the stuff come from what'd you say?"

Gussie thought back to the old days.

"They was sent to me by an aunt in Baghdad."

Wilf had never heard this excuse before.

"Why Baghdad?"

Gussie made an expansive gesture.

"All happens in Baghdad and there everyone has an aunt."

Wilf's voice became stern.

"Well, you can say what you like as long as you don't

mention no names. If you do" – he made a gurgling sound and drew a finger across his throat – "you know what'll 'appen."

Gussie was charmed but felt Wilf had not quite finished the story.

"Then you throw my body in the ditch where I am eaten by hyenas."

Wilf blew a sharp whistle on his fingers and at once three of his friends rushed in. Wilf pointed to Gussie.

"The kid's joinin'. Stand round. Now, Gussie, you says after me, 'I swear to obey my leader Wilf whatever he tells me to do, and I swear even in the face of death I'll never give away the name of any member of The Gang.' Anyone got a knife?"

A rather rusty knife was produced and Gussie was told to hold out his wrist. Then one of his friends made a nick on it and a nick in his own wrist and, when spots of blood appeared, rubbed them together.

"Now you are a blood brother," said Wilf, "but before you gets taught the sign you 'ave to do a test."

"Yes, I know," Gussie agreed. "Tom said I would have to. What must I do?"

The same cunning smile came over Wilf's face.

"In your uncle's garden isn't there a couple of gnomes?"

Gussie was surprised.

"I never knew they were called gnomes but there are two little men who fish. How did you know they were there? You can't see them from the road."

"You'd be surprised what I know," said Wilf. "and maybe you can 'elp me to know more, there's lots interesting about The Crescent. Now what you 'as to do is to fetch one of those gnomes an' bring it to me here. When I 'ave the gnome you're in."

"And then can I sell things and start to earn some money?" Gussie asked.

Wilf smiled his cunning smile.

"I don't know about sellin'. I might have other work for you. But when you brings that gnome I shouldn't wonder if you could 'ave fifty pence on account like."

Gussie was so cock-a-hoop at having succeeded in one try in joining The Gang that it was not until he was walking home from school that it got through to him how terribly difficult a task he had been set. A gnome might, for all he knew, be heavy. Then, even if he could take a gnome without The Uncle catching him, how was he to carry it to school? It was the kind of thing everybody would notice.

With a kind of turning-over feeling in his inside Gussie faced the awful fact that he might not be able to do his test. Perhaps Wilf had purposely set him something he couldn't do. It was a terrible thought for it meant if he did not bring a gnome to school he couldn't join The Gang so couldn't get any money.

The children were supposed to walk home together, but there was no one to see that they did and no one to complain if they did not so quite often Francesco and Anna walked together and Gussie loitered behind, skylarking with the other boys. This day he deliberately stayed behind because he was so full of thoughts about the gnome that he wanted to be alone.

The route The Crescent children used going to and from school crossed a busy road where a lollipop lady was waiting to see them safely across. The lights were red, so Gussie lolled against a lamp-post waiting for them to change and the lollipop lady to signal him over. While he stood there saying in his head "Suppose I could borrow a gnome without The Uncle seeing, how could I get it to school without anybody noticing?" he was distracted by what to him was an unusual sight. Two children came along pulling a strange figure in a sort of cart made of a box. It was wearing a mask and an old hat. While he was staring at the cart, the lollipop lady caught hold of him.

"Come on, dreamer. I've been signalling and signalling you to cross but you took not a bit of notice."

Gussie pointed to the figure sitting in the little cart.

"What's that?"

The lollipop lady led Gussie into the road and held up the traffic.

"That's a penny for the guy, of course. I'll be glad when the fifth of November's over. Blessed nuisance you kids are with your guys."

Safely across the road, Gussie gazed back at the little cart now disappearing round a corner. "A penny for the guy? The fifth of November? Blessed nuisance you kids are with your guys!" If other children could make little men and pull them about in carts why couldn't a gnome travel in the same way.

In a moment Gussie was cock-a-hoop again. He would ask Wally what a guy was. He was as good as in The Gang. He gave a hop, skip and a jump and ran home to tea.

24. The Gnome

ALTHOUGH THE DOCKSAY children were now part of the community, Wally still kept a proprietary eye on them all. So when the next morning in break he met Gussie looking for him he at once found a corner where they could talk.

"How is the fifth of November?" Gussie asked.

"Not ''ow is?' You say 'what is?' It's about the gunpowder treason and plot. There was this bloke called Guy Fawkes and 'e tried to blow up the 'Ouses of Parliament but they caught 'im at it. And ever since we make guys and burns them on bonfires on the fifth of November, which was the day he tried to do it. Then there's always fireworks."

"Can anybody make a guy?"

"Course. I sometimes makes one. I lug it around in the pram and asks people for a penny for the guy. The money what you get is to buy the fireworks." Then Wally remembered that Gussie had not yet got his share of Anna's dancing lesson money. "But if you was to get given any you could use it for Anna, nobody wouldn't know."

Gussie could not confide in Wally, for he had a feeling he might disapprove of Wilf and of his joining The Gang. Yet he had to have the pram and that he wanted it had to be a secret.

"Could you lend me the pram just for tonight? I'll get it back to you before school tomorrow. And could you not tell anyone you were lending it? You see, I want to surprise Francesco when I give him fifty pence."

"Fat chance you got of gettin' fifty pence," said Wally. "You'll be doing wonderful if you get ten. People don't give like they did, they say that fireworks is dangerous and us kids shouldn't be allowed to beg."

"But is it permitted?"

"The p'lice don't stop you if that's what you mean, but me dad would wallop me if he knew I took out a guy. 'Im and me mum don't 'old with it."

All Gussie needed to know was that it was not a police offence. Of course The Uncle would be angry if he knew one of his gnomes was being shown as a guy, but that had to be risked.

"Could I borrow the pram tonight?"

Wally was doubtful.

"Why don't I come along of you? Me mum won't 'alf be after me if she 'ears you been down town on your own after dark an' that."

Gussie could be very persuasive.

"All I want is to fetch the pram after tea, push it around for not more'n an hour I should think, then I'll bring it back to you."

Grudgingly Wally agreed.

"Well, you know where it stands, at the back of Bess's sty. But for goodness' sake walk quiet. You 'aven't seen me mum when she's creatin' and believe me you don't want to."

All the rest of the day Gussie worked on his plan. Teacher after teacher scolded him for inattention but Gussie didn't care. What he had to do was desperately important and needed careful working out; let them scold, he would attend to his lessons tomorrow.

That day after tea Gussie, without saying a word to Francesco or Anna, slipped out of the house. He knew it was a safe thing to do for though Francesco might worry he wouldn't say anything to The Aunt and of course, nobody, unless they had to, ever spoke to The Uncle.

Gussie's first objective was the pram. Usually the things from the stall were left in it overnight covered with a sheet of plastic, but Wally had promised to clear it out so that there would be room for the guy.

It felt funny creeping through Wally's farm without calling out "Hi! Can I come in?" Especially as the telly was blaring out to show the family were at home. It felt awful to sneak up behind Bess's sty without saying a word or giving her a scratch, and Bess thought so too for she seemed to recognize Gussie's smell for she gave him a surprised grunt. The pram, being old and squeaky, would not have been easy to move quietly, but luckily any noise it made was drowned out by the pop music being belted out from the TV set.

Gussie, without attracting anyone's attention, pushed the pram up The Crescent and quietly parked it outside Dunroamin. Now came the difficult part. Each house in The Crescent had a little path on one side of the house with a gate at the far end, beyond which stood the dustbins which were emptied once a week. Cecil always entered his garden through the French windows in the lounge, so he kept the gate into his garden locked except on the day when the dustmen came. This was not the dustmen's day so Gussie knew the gate would not be open. But Mr Allan, father of the twins, had no French windows so he and his family always came into their garden through the gate. Gussie, knowing this, nipped up their garden path and down into their garden.

It felt strange seeing Dunroamin from the wrong side of the wall. The lights were on in their bedrooms so Francesco and Anna were doing their homework, though more likely Anna was doing her dancing. He stood on tiptoe to peer over the wall and saw what he had expected. The curtains in the lounge were drawn, so there was no chance The Uncle could see out, and most likely The Aunt was in the kitchen cooking supper. Now all he had to do was climb over the wall.

All he had to do! The wall was straight up and with no footholds and, because there had recently been rain, a little slippery. It was then that Gussie thought of the dustbins. Standing on a dustbin he could reach the top of the wall and haul himself over. Dustbins had played no part in the children's lives before the earthquake, but they had studied them since and were filled with admiration.

"Such a system!" Francesco had marvelled when first catching the dustmen at work. "All carried away so no smell and no mess."

Gussie went to examine the Allans' dustbins. There were two, they were large and made of metal with plastic tops. But what Gussie had not suspected from the easy way the dustmen handled the bins was that they were heavy and it was only by slow stages that he managed to get one to the wall. Then, very out of breath, he climbed on to the plastic lid.

Plastic dustbin lids do not always fix on securely, they get warped by wind and rain. The Allans' dustbin had a lid like that. As a result when Gussie climbed on to the lid it tipped up, and down Gussie fell with a terrible clatter.

At once the curtains of the Allans' lounge window were drawn back and the window was opened. Two people hung out and a voice Gussie recognized as Jonathan's asked:

"Who's there?"

It was obvious to Gussie that it was no good trying to hide from the twins so he ran over to the window.

"It's me, Gussie," he whispered. "I fell off your dustbin."

The twins were full of curiosity.

"Whatever were you doing on our dustbin?" Priscilla asked.

"Ssh!" whispered Gussie. "Don't let anyone hear. If you come out I'll tell you."

The Gnome

The twins were supposed to be doing their homework but they never bothered with it much and often, especially in the summer, would climb out of the window into the garden. They climbed out now.

While they were climbing out Gussie made a quick decision. He would tell the twins what he was going to do but not about Wilf or joining The Gang.

"I was going to climb the wall to take one of The Uncle's gnomes."

The twins thought that a splendid idea. "Where are you taking it to?"

"I thought the school," said Gussie. "I have borrowed a perambulator, it will look like a penny for the guy."

"But the school's shut. Where will you put it?" Priscilla asked.

Gussie had not thought that far. "I suppose I could hide it somewhere."

Jonathan started to giggle. "Why hide it? Let's put it on the head's window ledge. It's quite large and the gnome could fish into the flower bed underneath the window."

Gussie thought about that. It was true Wilf had said bring the gnome in to him, but he couldn't really expect that for how could anyone carry a gnome to school without being seen? It was a joyous thought to put it on the head's window ledge, and even more gorgeous that Jonathan meant to help.

"All right. Can you help me on to the dustbin?"

Jonathan and Priscilla held the dustbin lid in place and Gussie, now able to reach the top of the wall, hauled himself over. On the other side he lowered himself quietly into the garden, landing on some plastic chrysanthemums. Very quietly he fumbled his way towards the gnomes.

Always Gussie had supposed the gnomes would be very heavy so he nearly spoilt everything by using too much strength to pick one up, with the result that he fell into the pool with the gnome on top of him. Luckily the lounge curtains were thick and the windows were shut, so Cecil did not hear the splash, but Jonathan and Priscilla did and in a few seconds Jonathan was hauling first the gnome and then Gussie out of the pond.

"Come on quick," he said. "I can get up the wall. Then pass the gnome up to me. Priscilla will take it, then I'll pull you up."

Except that Gussie was very wet and his teeth chattering with cold it was all too easy. Mrs Allan was cooking on the other side of the house, and Mr Allan was out for the evening. In a matter of minutes the gnome, with his fishing rod, which they discovered was detachable, lying beside him, was in the pram. Priscilla had fetched her own and Jonathan's coats and a warm sweater for Gussie and they and the pram were halfway up The Crescent.

"Now the only place we have to be careful is crossing the main road," said Jonathan. "You better leave saying 'a penny for the guy' to me and Priscilla because we know how."

"But if we get any pennies we can't keep them," Priscilla pointed out. "Dad wouldn't mind about the gnome, he'd think it funny, but he'd be livid if we took charity money, so if we get any we'll put it in somebody's collecting box." As it happened nobody gave the children any money but neither did they pay any attention to them, there were too many guys about.

The school gate was locked but Jonathan climbed over and Priscilla passed him the gnome, then she and Gussie climbed over. The school grounds seemed very eerie that night for there were no lights in the grounds, but the twins knew their way perfectly. The only disappointment was that, having set up the gnome on his window ledge, it was too dark to see him.

"And remember," Priscilla warned, "you can't go and look at him tomorrow, Gussie. We can only go when somebody else tells us he's there. Nobody must ever know who put him there."

Outside the school grounds Gussie collected the pram and said goodnight to the twins, then he went off towards Wally's farm pushing the pram. When he got to the farm it seemed as if he had only been away five minutes. It sounded as if the same tune was roaring out from the TV and Bess gave the same surprised grunt. But Gussie did not feel the same. He'd done it. He'd taken The Uncle's gnome. Tomorrow he'd be a proper member of The Gang. Goodness, he felt proud! When he got home, in answer to Francesco's anxious questions, all he would say was:

"You find out what 'a penny for the guy' means. That's all I'll tell you."

25. Call the Police

THE NEXT MORNING the three children went off to school as usual, but they were not inside the school gates before they could feel something unusual had happened. All the school were milling around, shrieking with laughter and standing by the headaster's window ledge. Presently the headmaster looked out. He roared with laughter when he saw the gnome.

"He's an unexpected visitor. Do any of you know where the little gentleman has come from?"

The children made various suggestions but none near the truth.

"Well, I must see what I can find out. I don't love gnomes myself but no doubt somebody does and is missing this little fellow."

After roll call the headmaster signalled to the school not

to move. He was smiling, so evidently he still thought the gnome funny.

"Have any of you ever seen that gnome before?"

First Francesco's hand was held up, then Anna's and lastly Gussie's. Then, after a second, the twins put their hands up.

The headmaster looked at Francesco.

"Where have you seen the gnome?"

"It is The Uncle's," Francesco explained. "He has two who fish in a pond though there are no fish."

"And our visitor is one of the two?"

Francesco shook his head.

"He looks the same but perhaps all such gnomes look the same."

"And where have you two seen him?" the headmaster asked the twins.

"In Mr Docksay's garden," said Jonathan.

"We live next door," Priscilla explained.

"And you both think it's one of Mr Docksay's gnomes?"

Jonathan managed a realistic shrug of the shoulders.

"He looks the same."

The headmaster did not question Gussie or Anna.

"All right," he said. "I'll telephone Mr Docksay to see if a gnome is missing." Then, signalling to the pianist to start playing, he called out "School dismiss."

As it happened Cecil had not looked out of his windows that morning so he was very surprised at the headmaster's question on the telephone.

"A gnome! Hold on, Headmaster, I will look." A second

later Cecil was back on the telephone. "Indeed it is mine. Vandalism! I shall call the police."

"The gnome appears undamaged," said the headmaster calmly. "I think it must have been intended as a joke."

Cecil almost roared.

"A joke! A joke! Do you call it a joke when somebody breaks into the privacy of your garden?"

The headmaster felt he could do no good.

"Well, if you will drive up to the school I'll see the school keeper helps you lift the gnome into your car. I'm sorry this has happened."

Cecil shouted for Mabel who came scurrying down the stairs.

"Someone has had the impertinence to take one of my gnomes up to the school."

Mabel's hand flew to her mouth.

"Oh no!" she panted. "Whoever would do that?"

"Where were the children last night?"

"In their rooms doing their homework."

"You're sure?"

"Of course, dear. Anyway how could they get into the garden? You were in the lounge."

Cecil went to his desk and took out the key to the garden gate.

"And the gate was locked. Then someone got over the wall. I shall call the police."

Mabel gave a squeak.

"Must you, dear? I mean, if you know where it is there is

not much the police can do, is there?"

"It's vandalism. An Englishman's home should be his castle."

"Yes, dear. I suppose so, dear," Mabel agreed. "If you are going to telephone the police I'll finish making the beds."

At the top of the stairs Mabel paused to listen to make sure Cecil was on the telephone, then she hurried into the boys' room. From behind the wardrobe where Gussie had hidden them she took out some very damp clothes and a strange jersey. The jersey she folded nearby then put it in his drawer where he could not fail to see it, but the clothes she put into the washing machine.

Very naughty of him if he took it, she thought, but I don't see how he could have. Such a little boy to carry one of those large gnomes.

Cecil was not finding the police as helpful as expected.

"Yes, sir," the policeman at the end of the line was saying. "A gnome. I've got that. But it's been recovered, I think you said, sir, so what were you wanting us to do?"

"I want every inch of the garden examined to discover where someone broke in."

"Very well, sir. I'll tell the inspector."

"And I want your men here at once."

"I'll see what can be done," the policeman said placatingly. "Good morning, sir."

It was pouring with rain at break time so the children had to stay in. Anna was looking for Francesco or Gussie when she was caught by the arm by Doreen and dragged into a corner. Doreen was looking plumper than ever and her ringlets bobbed every time she spoke, but for once she was not giggling.

"What are you dancing in Miss de Veane's concert, Anna?"

Anna felt as if someone was squeezing her inside.

"I'm not dancing. Miss de Veane knows I cannot dance yet, I must have many years more training."

Doreen looked knowing.

"That's what you think but I'll tell you what we think. There's eight of us, with you, takes private lessons, and yesterday Miss de Veane gave us the designs of our costumes and told us what we were dancing in the fairy ballet. It's in a fairy wood and I'm a foxglove first and then a dragonfly, and all the others who learn private are flowers or a bee or that. The Saturday class are in groups – primroses and daisies and such. So we asked Miss de Veane who was to be the fairy what wakes all us flowers up and do you know what she said?"

Anna's eyes were dark with fright. This was her nightmare coming true.

"No," she whispered. "What?"

"Well, it was not said exactly – more hinted like. She said it was a very small girl who would one day be a beautiful dancer. Well, the only small one she teaches is you and my mum says it isn't fair. Here's me learnt since I was four so if anyone is to be picked out it should be me."

Anna could not think what to say for she knew that Miss de Veane could be very determined, even determined enough perhaps to make her dance when she did not want to. Then, almost as if he were beside her, she heard Jardek's whisper in his mixed Polish and English: "Anna, my Anna, you must live for nothing but to dance. Anything which comes between you and true dancing must be forgotten." In a flash Anna had changed. She was no longer afraid of Miss de Veane. She threw her chin into the air.

"If you wish to dance this fairy you should ask to do so. There is no thought that I will dance in public nor that I shall learn much longer with Miss de Veane. I am going to learn in London."

26. Trouble

WILF, THOUGH HE would not have dreamt of saying so, was amazed at the cleverness of Gussie. What an idea, he thought, having got the gnome to put it on the headmaster's window ledge. But what he admired most was Gussie's discretion.

"You mean to say," he asked, "that you never told young Wally why you wanted his pram?"

Gussie was surprised.

"Course not. You said what would happen if I told."

"Nor you didn't tell the Allan twins neither?"

"Course not. They just thought it was a funny thing to do. Actually it was Jonathan who thought how it would be to put the gnome on the headmaster's window ledge, and I thought the idea was fine because I couldn't bring it into the classroom."

"And you're dead sure your uncle won't guess you done it?"

"Why should he? He doesn't know about Wally's pram so how is he thinking I got the gnome to the school?"

"But Wally will guess why you wanted 'is pram."

Gussie dismissed that with a gesture.

"If he does he will not tell. He is our friend."

Wilf took two fifty-pence pieces from his pocket. He handed them to Gussie.

"There's plenty more where that came from. In a day or two I'll 'ave another job for you. But remember, you never say nothin' or…"

Gussie drew his finger across his throat with a blood-curdling noise.

"Then I am in a ditch being eaten by hyenas."

Wilf whistled for one of his friends.

"Show young Gussie the pass sign. He's in."

Gussie planned his great moment for showing Francesco and Anna his pound carefully. It was so clever of him to have earned it he must make an occasion of showing the other two that he had it. Should he just walk in and throw the money down or should he give it to Anna with a grand gesture, saying: "Here is your dancing-class money."

After school Wally joined Gussie.

"Walk a bit of the way 'ome with me. I want a word with you."

Gussie, still very much above himself for his tremendous success with Wilf, was charmed for he was sure Wally was going to tell him how clever and funny he had been, but Wally was not. As they walked along in the rain he suddenly burst out:

"I don't know nothin' about why you wanted the pram 'an I don't want'er know nothin' but anyone what joins up with Wilf's gang wants 'is 'ead seein' to."

Gussie tried to sound puzzled.

"How is Wilf's gang?"

"Come off it. D'you think nobody don't see what's goin' on? Everybody knows about The Gang though most is too scared to speak up. D'you think I don't know you was alone with Wilf dinner time? I shouldn't wonder if taking the gnome up in the pram wasn't something to do with it."

"Why should Wilf want the gnome?"

Wally was fond of Gussie but just now he could have shaken him.

"I can't do no more than warn you like. That Wilf is up to no good, I don't know what 'e does for I don't go near 'im and you wouldn't if you 'ad any sense. I know you want money for Anna's dancin' but if you take any from Wilf you'll be sorry. I know you're scared to do it but it would be better to ask your uncle."

"Him! He will not give, especially for dancing which he says is a sin. Anyway, he has a closed purse."

Wally kicked a stone up the road.

"I don't know what to say to you. I've told you to keep away from Wilf. I can't do not more not unless I was to tell me mum about you, an' I can't do that."

Gussie was furious with Wally for trying to spoil his glorious day. He did not want to hear bad things about Wilf for, somewhere pushed away inside him, was a sneaking suspicion that Wally was right.

"If you want to know, I was only talking to Wilf at dinner time about the gnome. He thought it very funny. And I'll talk to anybody I like an' you can't stop me."

As a result of this conversation with Wally, Gussie, instead of bursting with pride, came home cross. All the way home he had muttered to himself Christopher's favourite saying: "It's a crying scandal! It's a crying scandal!" He had no idea what it meant but it sounded good. However, once he was in The Crescent his spirits revived and he jingled his fifty-pence pieces together with pride.

In the house he rushed up the stairs and flung open his and Francesco's bedroom door. He was in luck, Anna was in the room. It was his big moment.

"Anna," he said. "You can stop fussing. Here is two more lessons and I will have another fifty pence whenever you want it."

It was Francesco who answered.

"Anna will no longer work with Miss de Veane. She says she must go to London to this Madame Scarletti."

Could anything be more infuriating? To have succeeded in joining The Gang just to pay for dancing classes. To have stolen a gnome so cleverly and to have made the entire school laugh. To come home with a whole pound just to be told Anna did not want it. This was too much. With a crimson face Gussie turned on Anna.

"Always there is something. First it is shoes. Then it is

classes. Then it is tunic, now you have all except enough money to pay until S'William gets home. Then, when first Francesco and then me get the money, all you say is now you must go to London to this Madame Scarletti. Well, you cannot go, for even if you could see Madame Scarletti once that is all, for how can you go each week to London?"

Francesco looked anxiously at the door. "Do be quiet, Gussie, or The Uncle will hear and you know he does not like noise. Anna cannot learn from Miss de Veane because she will make her dance as a fairy on a stage in public."

"Well, let her be a fairy then. For just one day it will do no harm. But London is impossible."

Anna could hear Jardek speaking.

"You know I cannot dance in public or do anything but exercises. Jardek said…"

"Jardek said! Jardek said!" Gussie roared. "But Jardek is dead."

Francesco turned to Anna. "Gussie's quite right. If Jardek was here now he would see it is not possible you should go to London."

"And he would see you must dance this fairy," Gussie added.

The door opened and Aunt Mabel looked in.

"Oh, please be quiet, dears. I can hear you all over the house. Fortunately your uncle is out, for if he was in he would be most annoyed." She sidled into the room. "I was going to warn you to be very quiet at supper. Your uncle is angry with the police. He is seeing a superintendent now."

There was a moment's shocked silence. All three children knew about police. Too often had police moved on the caravan. In some countries police would be pacified with money but that was unlikely in Britain.

"What has The Uncle done?" Francesco asked.

"Nothing, dear, of course," Mabel puffed. "It is that gnome. You will have heard about it at school. The police came to find out which way somebody got into the garden."

Gussie felt as if cold water was trickling down his spine. "And did they find out?"

"That's what your uncle is so angry about. They came so late that the rain had washed away all the marks. There was one chrysanthemum bent but the police did not think that was evidence."

Gussie released a deep breath. Francesco said:

"We will be very careful not to offend at supper."

The children did not speak for a moment or two after Mabel had sidled out of the room. Then Francesco said:

"You had better go to your room, Anna, to get tidy for supper." Then, when Anna had gone, he turned to Gussie. "I do not know what you are doing but even for Anna's dancing you should not do what is wrong. Jardek would not wish that."

Now that Gussie knew the police had not discovered how he had got into the garden he was his old self again.

"When you got one pound fifty pence did I say you had done what was wrong? No. But you look at my pound as if I am a thief. Now I will tell you a secret, it was me borrowed the silly old gnome but I did not hurt him so leave me alone."

27. A Load of Worries

FRANCESCO WAS SO full of worries he began to look quite ill. His biggest worry was Gussie, for Wally had told him about his suspicions.

"I know he doesn't look very nice, but what is it bad that this Wilf is doing?"

Wally tried to explain.

"Nobody outside his gang don't know nothin', not for sure, but he's always givin' little kids thin's to sell."

"In Britain that is wrong?" Francesco asked.

"Course not, if they're come by honest, but what they say is they're pinched." He saw Francesco did not understand. "Stole like."

Francesco was shocked.

"Stole! To steal is a sin."

Wally thought he might have exaggerated.

"If not stole they're come by funny, what's called rejects from a factory what someone's got 'old of. Anyway, you don't want young Gussie mixed up in anything like that."

Francesco agreed fervently. Too well he knew how easily Gussie might get mixed up in something bad, not because he was bad but because, like Christopher, he liked excitement.

"I do not know what I can do," he told Wally. "Because I am the eldest, now almost eleven, I can try to look after Gussie and Anna, but it is hard to be Jardek, Babka, Christopher and Olga all together. You see, there is only me now."

Wally wondered if he should have bothered Francesco.

"I wouldn't get into a state about it. After all, we don't know, not for certain, about Wilf's gang. But it wouldn't do no 'arm to keep an eye open and if you see young Gussie selling anythin' then you can do somethin'. Maybe go to the headmaster."

Go to the headmaster! Francesco classed him with The Uncle. To talk to either was impossible.

"Thank you for telling me," he said. Then he turned away so that Wally never knew there were tears in Francesco's eyes.

Then there was Anna. Anna, so good and gentle until there was interference in her dancing. Francesco did not believe that S'William had let them down. Gussie's idea that he had stolen their picture was fantastic. On the other hand he certainly was being slow coming home.

If only S'William would arrive, Francesco thought, it would be as if a great stone rolled off his back, for S'William was the kind of man who took charge and saw no difficulties anywhere. Never would Francesco forget the way he had said to Anna: "Nonsense. You can't live in a hospital tent for ever. You have been given into my charge for the time being and I don't intend to let you out of my sight until I see you settled."

Of course, from S'William's point of view, that was just what had happened. He had found them an uncle and an aunt and they had good clothes and, though often nasty, especially cabbage, plenty to eat. All in fact should have been well. How could S'William know that in their school there would be Wilf and his gang? How could he know that Miss de Veane should wish Anna to dance in public? How could he know the trouble he had caused by writing about Madame Scarletti?

What Francesco supposed had happened was that S'William, for reasons to do with is work, had delayed coming home and, if he thought about them at all, supposed they were safe and well. In any case he might think they were old enough to look after themselves for all their birthdays were near Christmas, which meant he would soon be eleven, Gussie ten and Anna nine. Perhaps in Britain at such ages you were no longer considered a child.

The next Wednesday Anna went to her dancing class with her plans clearly made.

"I shall say nothing," she promised Francesco, "unless she tries to teach me a dance. Then I shall say 'no' – exercises only. I pay so I decide."

"Try not to finish with Miss de Veane," Francesco begged. "Some day you shall see this Madame Scarletti, but not now, and in Fyton Miss de Veane is all that there is."

Outside the studio it was bitterly cold, with a fine stinging rain in the wind. This gave Francesco an idea.

"Perhaps," he said, "as it is so cold I could come inside."

Anna was not sure she liked that suggestion.

"It is not a very big studio."

"But it is so cold," Francesco pleaded. "Already my teeth knock together."

Anna was very cold herself but Francesco looked blue, so she relented.

"Come in. I will ask."

Anna went across the studio and gave her bob.

"Today is so cold," she said, "is it permitted my brother stays inside while he waits to take me home?"

Miss de Veane gave Anna what was meant to be a friendly smile but actually looked more like the smile the wolf gave Red Riding Hood.

"Of course, dear. Now, hurry away and change for I have something new for you to learn."

Francesco gazed spellbound at Miss de Veane. Her orange-coloured hair with black roots. Her black dress which was far too tight over the chest and hips, though it did finish up in a short pleated skirt so that she could dance, though how anyone could dance in white boots Francesco could not imagine. He thought of Jardek in his neat blouse and full trousers with his violin tucked under his chin and felt sick.

Poor Anna, he thought. Even though perhaps the teaching is good she cannot like working with this lady.

Quite soon Anna was back. Mabel had made her a very neat tunic and she looked charming in it with her plaits pinned up on top of her head. She went straight to the barre, held on to it and turned out her feet.

"No, dear," said Miss de Veane. "We are not starting with exercises today. I have an enchaînement I want you to learn."

Anna did not move.

"What for?"

Miss de Veane hesitated, it was clear she was not used to having her orders questioned, but eventually she decided to make Anna an exception.

"We, that is all the children in my little school, are going to try to raise enough money to buy a guide dog for a blind person. We are giving a dancing matinée. The ballet, which is half the programme, takes place in a fairy wood in which live many flowers. A fairy dances through the wood to wake the flowers. You would not mind being the fairy to help a blind person, would you?"

Anna did not move or change the position of her feet.

"Of course I would wish to help the blind. Always when we lived in a caravan we saw many, many blind and always Christopher gave money. But I will not dance this fairy, there is much work I must do before I can dance such a role."

"That, I think," said Miss de Veane, her hoarse voice sounding as if she had chipped ice in her throat, "is for me to decide."

Anna shook her head.

"No – me. It has been hard for my brothers to earn the money for my lessons, but it has been earned so now it is I who decide what I will learn and I do not dance that solo."

Miss de Veane would not have allowed any other pupil to speak to her like that. She was only allowing it now because she knew that in Anna she had something as precious as a jewel. If could be persuaded to dance she would dance well for she was incapable of dancing badly. Then one look at Anna dancing and every mum in the audience would think, if I sent my Sally or Marlene or Caroline to learn dancing she will dance like that. So, swallowing her temper which made her feel as if she was swallowing red hot coals, she said:

"I think you are forgetting the blind person, dear, who is waiting for a guide dog."

Francesco did not know what a guide dog was so he was sure Anna did not. He got up and came over to Anna and Miss de Veane. He gave Miss de Veane a little bow.

"Always we have lived abroad where such dogs are not. Perhaps if you could tell Anna about such a dog she will understand."

Miss de Veane had a desk in the corner of studio. She went to it and took out a folder. On the front was a picture of a splendid Alsatian wearing his special guide dog harness. She gave the folder to the children.

"Imagine, if you were blind, what it would mean to you to be looked after by a dog like that."

Both the children were most impressed.

"We never had a dog," said Francesco, "only our horse, he was called Togo. It would be wonderful to have a dog, Anna, to lead you if you were blind."

But Anna was not to be moved by pity.

"It is good a blind person should have such a dog," she agreed. "The blind we have known are looked after by the children of the family but maybe a dog is better. But my dancing will not buy a dog, some other pupil will dance the fairy. But because the dog is needed I will ask The Aunt to buy a ticket."

Francesco and Miss de Veane exchanged looks.

Francesco's look said: "I'm afraid it's no good asking her but please go on teaching her for I do not know how to get her to London." Miss de Veane's look said, "See what you can do to make your sister dance, for if she refuses I shall not teach her and then what will you do?"

28. Plans

The next week was the half-term holiday. Wally had explained this to the Docksays and so had most of the children living in The Crescent, for of course walking to and from school nobody paid any attention to Cecil's silly rules so they were all friends. The only rule the children kept was not accepting invitations for tea and television – that, in their own street, was asking for trouble.

"We're goin' away," Wally had told Francesco. "But we'll be back at the weekend so Mum says she'll expect you Saturday and Sunday same as usual.

"Where are you going to?" Francesco asked.

"Me dad's sister, my auntie that is. Lives in London, she does. It's interestin' where she hangs out because it's near the river an' I watches them loadin' an' unloadin' the ships."

Francesco, as Wally told him this, felt a horrible wave of

unhappiness sweep over him. In his mind he was in Turkey. Christopher was trying to get a curious light effect he said he could only find on the Bosphorus. Olga was having trouble with police who wanted the caravan moved. Olga could not give lessons because of arguing with the police, so he, Gussie and Anna had gone to the waterside and watched the ships. They had remembered they had some money so they had climbed into a boat which was going to the Golden Horn. At the end of their journey they had bought cakes and ice cream and made friends with a dancing bear and listened to the muezzin calling the faithful to prayer, a real proper muezzin – not one of those gramophone records which made Christopher swear. Nothing special happened. They took another boat home where they found Christopher having drinks with the police. It was just one of those days which, from England on a grey November morning, made a lump come into your throat.

"Me dad was saying maybe you three would see to Bess and the hens while we was away. Mum'll show you where we keeps the key. It's only Tuesday to Friday, for we'll see to them Monday before we goes."

All the children loved Wally's farm so naturally Francesco agreed.

"It will be nice to have something to do for of course we will go nowhere."

Other people beside Wally had plans for the half-term. Tom, looking rather like a scared white mouse wearing glasses, sidled up to Gussie in the morning break to whisper:

"Wilf wants to see you dinner time. Same place as before."

Gussie was delighted. He had been disappointed in The Gang. He thought once he had joined them life would be full of excitement but nothing had happened at all. So at dinner time he almost ran to the senior classroom, only pausing to give a good dramatic version of the pass sign. Wilf, looking dirtier and more scruffy than usual, was sitting at his desk.

"Shut the door," he told Gussie, "for what I got to say is special private."

Gussie shut the door then stood expectantly beside Wilf waiting for orders.

"What I'm plannin' will be a bit of fun like for the 'alf-term."

Gussie was delighted, he was all in favour of fun.

"What am I to do?"

Wilf chose his words carefully.

"There's many more what belongs to The Gang than what you see in this school. Some's quite old — maybe twenty an' more. Well, I was telling them of the way you brought your uncle's gnome to the school and they wouldn't believe it."

"Well, it was difficult," Gussie boasted, "and nobody but me ever knew why I took it to the school. You ought to have seen The Uncle. He was terribly angry and sent for the policemen."

Wilf nodded.

"Well, next Tuesday will be dead easy, I'm bringing two of the leaders like to see the gnomes, they thought they'd paint them different colours."

Gussie giggled.

"I cannot imagine The Uncle when he sees them changed. I think he could explode like a firework. How will you get in?"

"Now listen careful," said Wilf, "for I don't like sayin' things twice. Can you find a way to stay awake?"

"I never tried," Gussie admitted, "but I expect I could find a way."

"You don't 'ave to find no way for I've got it. You ties a long piece of string to your big toe and 'angs it out of the winder, then when we gets there I gives it a pull."

"But how have you got into the garden?" Gussie asked.

"Same way as you did. Through the gate and over the twins' wall."

"When I am awake what do I do?" Gussie asked.

"You sneak down the stairs and comes out into the garden to 'elp paint the gnomes."

"Through the lounge, you mean. This will be easy."

"That's right," Wilf agreed. "I told you it was dead easy. Now let's see you got it right."

Gussie took a deep breath.

"Next Tuesday before I go to sleep I tie a long piece of string to my toe and hang the end out of the window. That is easy for my bed is by the window. In the night you pull the string, I wake up and creep very, very quietly down into the hall and through the lounge into the garden where you will be painting the gnomes."

Wilf sounded pleased.

"You got it."

"What colour shall the gnomes be?"

Wilf smiled his cunning smile.

"We've not gone into that, not yet. Suppose you choose."

Gussie was flattered.

"I think bright blue would be nice."

"Blue it is," Wilf agreed. "And I don't 'ave to remind you not one word of this to anybody."

"Not one word," Gussie agreed, "or…" and he drew a finger across his throat, and made a bloodthirsty noise.

Anna was not happy after the dancing class at which Francesco was present for she did not feel that he understood. Walking home he had told her how wonderful for a person who was blind it must be to have a dog. How perhaps just one dance would not hurt. He did not speak about Jardek in words for he hated to do, but underneath all he did say was: "If Jardek was here now I think he would understand." On one point Anna found Francesco did agree with her. He thought Miss de Veane terrible.

"I wish," he had said, "that it was possible to take you to the Madame Scarletti, but for this I think we must wait for S'William."

Anna did not feel she could wait for anyone. If someone who was the best dancer in the world said they would teach her then nobody, not even The Uncle who thought to dance was a sin, could stop her from learning.

It was a terrible thing, Anna considered, for her to act on her own. This was something which before the earthquake had never happened. But now it had to happen. Francesco and Gussie would not agree so she must go to London alone to see Madame Scarletti. She knew where the money was for the fare. Under the paper beside S'William's address. Next week when there was a holiday she would take the money and, carrying her shoes and tunic in a bag, she would visit this Madame Scarletti and ask her to watch her work.

29. Madame Scarletti

ON THE TUESDAY Gussie woke up feeling very happy and above himself. It would be such fun to get up in the middle of the night. It made him want to laugh out loud when he thought of The Uncle's face in the morning. It also made him feel proud that two gang leaders were coming to see how one boy had carried a gnome all the way to school.

Mabel was trying to make the half-term pleasant.

"Your uncle will be very busy all day," she told the children. "As you know, he's treasurer to various charities and today he has to divide a lot of money up which people get at Christmas." Mabel puffed after so long a speech. "So I thought you'd like to have your lunch out and then go to a film. I will give you a pound but your uncle must not know."

Francesco and Gussie liked the idea of lunch out. In Fyton there was a Chinese restaurant called The Lotus Bud and they had wanted to eat there ever since they came to live in The Crescent.

"For I bet they never have cabbage," Gussie had said.

Surprisingly it was Anna who was not keen to try The Lotus Bud.

"I wish to practise my dancing," she explained.

Gussie looked at her in disgust.

"You are getting to be a very tiresome girl," he told her. "You can't practise dancing all through the day, you must eat somewhere."

"Suppose Gussie and I go out this morning and feed Bessie and the hens then come back to fetch you to this Lotus Bud," Francesco suggested.

Anna did not look as if she liked the idea, but she said grudgingly:

"Very well. But not too early. The Aunt must finish my room before I can practise."

Francesco and Gussie went to the farm soon after breakfast. Bessie seemed delighted to see them for she was evidently missing her family. The boys tried to think the hens were pleased to see them too but they knew really that they were not.

"I think perhaps hens do not need friends," Francesco said, "which is a pity."

Doing the farm took quite a long time for Bessie had to have a warmed-up mixture to eat, and there were the eggs to collect and of course the hens to be fed. All the time they were working while Gussie was jabbering away about anything which came into his head, Francesco was uneasy. He could not think why but he felt unhappy about Anna. Why had she decided she must practise that morning? She was hiding something, he was sure of it.

"Come on, Gussie," he said. "Let's lock up and then we can fetch Anna."

Gussie was surprised.

"She won't be ready yet. I do not think The Aunt has even finished her room. Let's stay here and turn on the telly."

"We cannot do that," Francesco said firmly. "We don't know how and they would not like it, and anyway I do not think there are pictures in the morning."

Gussie scowled.

"Always nowadays you are saying 'No! No! No!' all the time. You never used to do this."

Francesco was sorry.

"I am the eldest and someone must say it. You know Wally's dad would not wish us to touch his telly."

Gussie did know, but he did not want to hear about it.

"Then let's go down in town, there's sure to be some boys from the school about."

Francesco shook his head.

"You do as you wish, but me I am going to fetch Anna. I do not mind waiting until she is ready. I will bring her to The Lotus Bud at half past twelve."

Gussie did not mind a morning on his own. If he met some of his friends they might have fun.

"OK," he said. "And you can go now if you wish. I will lock up."

The key to the Walls' house lived under a grating near the pigsty. All three children knew where it lived but Francesco was officially in charge of it.

"You promise you will put the key in the right place?"

Gussie was insulted.

"Of course I will. Nobody but you is so sure I will not do things I should."

Francesco was ashamed.

"I know and I am sorry but somehow in Britain I feel there is only me, at least until S'William comes back. That makes me say 'no' when I do not mean it."

Francesco, without meaning to, ran almost all the way back to Dunroamin. He could hear The Aunt in the kitchen and knew The Uncle would be counting money behind the shut lounge door. He ran quietly up the stairs, meaning to go to Anna's room, but instead he stood on the top of the stairs staring into his and Gussie's room. The door was open and so was the door of the wardrobe in which they kept S'William's address, his letter and their money. Anna, dressed to go out, was kneeling in front of the wardrobe taking from under the lining paper S'William's letter and their money, and putting both into a paper carrier bag which was lying beside her.

Francesco moved into the doorway.

"Anna! What are you doing?"

It was almost as if Anna had expected interference and was prepared for it. She stood up holding the carrier bag in her arms.

"I go to London to see Madame Scarletti. She must see

me dance. If she cannot see what Jardek saw then I will dance that fairy to buy a dog for someone who is blind. If she can see then she will teach me. This is sure."

"How were you going?"

"I go to the railway where I buy one ticket, it is called day return half price. Priscilla, who lives next door, told me this."

Francesco could see it was no good arguing.

"Then I will go too. I have here the pound The Aunt gave. But I have told Gussie to meet us at The Lotus Bud at twelve-thirty and he has no money."

Anna seemed pleased to have Francesco's company.

"Gussie will find money when he needs it. That is how Gussie is."

As it happened Gussie only looked in at The Lotus Bud to tell the other two he would not be staying for lunch. He had been invited to friends and there would be television afterwards. Not finding Francesco and Anna in the restaurant he rejoined his friends and thought no more about them.

Even if you knew London well, 45 Bemberton Street, Chelsea, was not easy to find. It was a little street tucked in amongst other streets, so close to the Thames you could hear the tugs hooting. Francesco and Anna never would have found it on their own. Fortunately for them, Christopher had often dropped bits of information about Britain into his conversation and one was: "Nothing to touch an English bobby if you want help." And then he would sing "If you want to know the time ask a policeman." So at the station when they arrived they had found a policeman and showed him S'William's letter and had been told to get to Sloane Square on the Underground, and then to take a bus to Chelsea Town Hall.

"When you get there," the policeman had said, "ask again."

So at the Town Hall they had asked again. They chose an old man selling newspapers.

"Funny you should ask me," he said, " 'cause I don't suppose many about here knows where it is." Then out of a pocket he took a piece of paper and a pencil and drew them a little map. "Stick to that an' you can't miss it. Foreign, aren't you?"

"Not now," Francesco explained. "Now we are British but it is not long we have lived here."

"You'll be all right in Bemberton Street," the paper man promised. "Proper United Nations up that way." Then he went back to selling his papers.

Bemberton Street was very shabby-looking. Paint was peeling off the wall, windows were cracked and so were the two steps leading to the front door of number 45. But to Anna the house was a fairy palace for in it lived Madame Scarletti. Francesco rang the bell, which was not answered, so he rang again. This time after a pause a grown-up girl wearing a black tunic and ballet shoes opened the door.

"We wish," Francesco said politely, "to see Madame Scarletti."

The girl looked amused.

"Many people wish to see Madame. They come from all over the world. But Madame sees no one without an appointment."

Francesco was appalled. He had agreed to the journey because Anna could not go alone, but it had not occurred to him that having got here Madame Scarletti would refuse to see them.

"Would you perhaps beg for us a few minutes, you see we come a long way and we will not have the money to do this twice. At least not till S'William gets home. Look!" He fumbled in his pocket and took out the envelope containing Sir William's letter. "You see, we are told to come here." He handed the girl the envelope and when she had opened the letter he pointed to the portion addressed to Anna.

The girl read what Sir William had written. Then she looked at the envelope, then turned it over and read "Sir William Hoogle" on the back.

"Docksay," she said. "Would you be the children Sir William Hoogle rescued after an earthquake?"

"We are two of them," Francesco agreed. "There is another called Gussie but he is not here."

The girl came to a decision. "Wait here. I will show Madame this letter."

It seemed to Francesco a long wait but Anna was not worried, she had reached Madame Scarletti's doorstep, it never crossed her mind she might get no further.

Anna was right to have faith. Presently the girl came back.

"Come along," she said. "Madame will see you."

Madame Scarletti was indeed very old but, as so often with dancers, she had kept her figure. She was small and looked as if she were made of frail porcelain. She had immense gleaming black eyes and her white hair was piled in intricate plaits on the top of her head. She was wearing a long taffeta dress and round her shoulders was a vivid scarlet shawl. On her feet were ballet shoes.

Madame Scarletti was sitting on a high-backed chair. Beside her was a long cane with an ivory top. Francesco and Anna approached her, then Francesco bowed and Anna, instead of her usual bob, made a lovely obeisance right down to the floor.

Madame Scarletti's voice was surprisingly strong for anyone so old. She looked only at Anna.

"Your father was Christopher Docksay."

Anna felt she ought to curtsey again but she didn't. "Yes, Madame."

"And he married Olga Popouska."

Anna looked at Francesco. "Was Olga called Popouska?" she asked him.

Francesco did not know. "I do not think we knew. She was just Olga and our father was Christopher, and our grandfather and grandmother were Jardek and Babka and our horse Togo."

"But I know," said Madame Scarletti. "Many, many years ago in Warsaw there was a great teacher of dancing. His name was Ivan Popouski. I did not know what happened to him until I read in a newspaper about the Turkish earthquake."

She turned to the girl in the black tunic. "This is Maria, my keeper and guardian, without whom I could not live. Did I not say to you, Maria, that the grandfather who was killed in the earthquake must be Ivan Popouski?"

"That's right," Maria agreed. "That's why I wanted you to see these two." She looked at Francesco and Anna. "Which is the dancer for I suppose one of you is?"

Madame made an impatient tch-tch-ing sound. She looked scornfully at Maria.

"Where are your eyes, girl? Do you not recognize the face of a dancer when you see one? I knew this little girl could dance the moment she entered the studio." Then she turned to Anna. "You have shoes with you?"

"And my tunic," Anna agreed.

Madame waved a hand gracefully towards the door. "Take the child where she can change."

Then she looked at Francesco. "Come and sit down." She pointed to a footstool. "I can see you have suffered. Tell me about it. Every small thing, it is much better not to shut things away inside, keep them outside where you can see them."

So Francesco told her. He started on the day of the earthquake. The terrible heat. The odd-looking yellowish sky.

"It was so hot that nobody is talking, and only because Olga said we must could we eat any breakfast – yoghourt and a slice of bread with black olives."

Then Francesco explained about the picture. How Christopher had said he would have taken it to the picture framer in the caravan but it would spoil Togo's holiday.

"You see, he was old and it would be a long way right across Turkey to the picture exhibition. Christopher could not take his picture to be framed because he must work. It was only three miles over the hill so we went. It was, I think, the only day when Jardek said it was too hot for Anna's dancing lesson."

Francesco paused there, seeing against the little house as they had last seen it, with Christopher, Olga, Jardek and Babka drinking tea.

After a moment Madame Scarletti gave him a friendly pat. "Go on. Every small thing. Lay it all out."

So Francesco went on. He described the terrible heat climbing over the hill so they were wet all over. How the picture framer was asleep on his bed so they had to leave the picture for him to see when he woke up. How they had bought figs, a leaf of mulberries and lemonade. How they had carried the food and drink halfway up the hill to picnic in the shade of some cacti. How it was then he noticed there were no birds. No birds at all. How Anna had told them the birds had left two days before, she had seen hundreds of them fly away.

There was another small pause while Francesco tried to remember. During this Anna, changed into her tunic, came back into the room with Maria. Francesco did not see them so Madame Scarletti put a finger to her lips and they quietly sat down.

"I think it was then Gussie saw the horse. As it seemed then it appeared to have gone mad, but I know now the horse knew just as the birds had known what was to happen, it was only us who did not know."

"Then it happened?" Madame Scarletti asked. Francesco nodded.

"In the camp, men asked us often how it was but we could not say. Now I can remember a great noise and hot air, then the earth moved and we were thrown everywhere. Afterwards we got to the top of the hill and looked. All was gone. The little house, Jardek, Babka, Christopher, Olga and Togo, as if they had never been."

Madame Scarletti seemed to know the end of the story.

"Then Sir William Hoogle found you and soon he discovered your uncle and your aunt with whom you are now living."

That was when Anna joined in. "They are not nice. The Uncle thinks to dance is wrong."

Francesco tried to be fair. "The Aunt tried to be kind but she is afraid of The Uncle. When S'William comes back I hope he will arrange things better."

Madame Scarletti beckoned to Anna. "Go to the barre and we will see what you have learnt." Then she smiled at Francesco.

"There is good news for you. Sir William has arrived in England. *The Times* newspaper printed this. Now he is home I believe you can be a little boy again."

30. Dial 999

MADAME SCARLETTI HAD a car. She told Maria to drive the children to the station and to see them on the right train.

"I shall write to Sir William," she told Francesco, "and arrangements will be made for Anna. It may be she will live here with me."

These words were like a Te Deum to Francesco. Madame would write to Sir William. Madame would make all the arrangements. Madame might even have Anna to live with her.

Because of being taken by car to the station, the children were home in good time, but Gussie was home before them. He had felt annoyed at this, for he wanted to tell them about a film he had seen on TV and he must do it before supper, for the last thing he wanted was Francesco and Anna being late going to bed. If he was to wake up in the middle of the night he should go to sleep early.

"Where have you been?" he demanded.

"To see Madame Scarletti," said Anna.

Anna spoke in so pleased a voice it maddened Gussie.

"And what for? Who is to pay for lessons in London?" Then he turned to Francesco. "Why did you let her go? It had been hard to get fifty pence for that Miss de Veane, to get enough for Madame Scarletti and to get Anna to London is impossible."

Francesco was too happy to mind what Gussie said.

"Imagine! S'William is in England. It is in *The Times* newspaper. Have you been to the farm to put Bessie and the hens to bed?"

Gussie would have loved to say "Yes, I have!" but he couldn't. Rushing home to tell the others about the television he had seen and the food he had eaten he had forgotten the farm in his annoyance at finding the other two out.

"No. But I will go now."

"Both will go now," said Francesco. "If we run we should not be back late for supper. But if we are, do not worry, Anna, keep saying 'S'William is back', then nothing The Uncle says will matter."

The boys ran all the way to the farm. It was dark when they got there so the hens were waiting to come into their coop. Bessie, of course, could get into her sty but there was a padlock on her door at night, the key of which was kept under the grating with the house key. Wally had lent them a torch.

"If S'William answers my letter soon," Francesco said, "have you a plan? I mean, we know about Anna but what about us? What do we want if the picture sells for much money?"

"I do not wish to live with The Uncle," said Gussie.

"I do not wish either," Francesco agreed. "But where else do we wish to go?"

Gussie fixed Bessie's lock.

"If it was possible I would like a caravan. Not of course as before – that can never be – or perhaps a little house like Babka and Jardek had, but I do not think that is possible in Britain. There will be police and laws about children living alone."

Francesco held out his hand for Bessie's key and turned the torch on to the grating.

"The only rule in Britain that we know is the one of which Christopher always spoke. Do you not remember how, if we made an extra noise when he was working, he would say 'I will have hush. If you kids lived where I was brought up I'd refuse to keep you, then they'd clap the lot of you into a home'?"

Gussie felt a sort of heave in his inside.

"Suppose The Uncle did not want us. Could he put us in a home?"

"Not unless we did something bad. But he does not have to have us. You remember how The Aunt said: 'He does not like children so it is hard for him that you are here, but he does his duty, he gives you a home.'"

Gussie, wondering if painting a gnome was so bad you could be clapped in a home said:

"And you said: 'We did not ask to come.' "

Francesco put away the keys.

"We are not going to do anything bad, but it is good that when we see S'William we tell him where it is we wish to live."

Gussie did not say much on the way back to Dunroamin. He wished now he had not agreed to paint a gnome blue, especially as there was no money in it, but it was too late now to do anything about it.

It had seemed to Gussie that evening that Francesco was never going to sleep. He was so excited about S'William coming home he had to talk about it. At last Gussie in desperation pretended to be asleep, in fact he pretended so well he was almost asleep when something reminded him of what he had to do. He sat up in bed and looked towards Francesco's bed. He certainly did seem to be asleep. Very quietly, Gussie slipped out of bed. The window was already open so, fixing a loop of the length of string Wilf had given him round his left big toe, he dropped the other end, which had a small weight on it, out of the window, got back into bed and promptly fell asleep.

What seemed to Gussie hours and hours later he was woken up by a continual tugging at his left toe. For a moment he could not remember what was happening, then it all came back to him. He felt down the bed for the string, took the loop off his toe, gave three tugs of the string as Wilf had told him, put on his dressing-gown and bedroom slippers and sneaked down the stairs. Very quietly he opened the lounge door, fumbled his way across the room to the French windows, unlocked them and he was in the garden. There he heard Wilf say "This is 'im." Then a sack was put over his head and he was rolled over on his face. Then once more he heard Wilf's voice.

"Now you lie still and nothin' won't 'appen to you. But if you tries anythin' you know what to expect."

Gussie, tied inside the sack, could not draw his finger across his throat but he knew all right. Just for a few moments he was puzzled. He expected to hear whispers and perhaps the movement of a pot of paint. He could not imagine why Wilf had tied him up in a sack instead of letting him paint one of the gnomes. Then a new thought came to him. Why was there no sound? Why did nobody move about, not even to give him a kick? The horrible answer soon came to him. The Gang were not wanting to paint a gnome. They had got him out into the garden so that he would leave the French windows open. They were going to steal from The Uncle.

The sack was uncomfortable and dirty but there was plenty of air inside it so Gussie could breathe. He rolled over on to his back and thought what to do. If he called for help Wilf and his friends would stop him, and anyway muffled in a sack The Uncle wouldn't hear, sleeping the other side of the house. But Gussie was agile as an eel. He rolled up and down the concrete paths, which pretended they were crazy paving, and at last he was rewarded, the rope which had held his arms to his sides shifted to his feet. Then it was a matter of seconds for Gussie to sit up, push off the rope and wriggle out of the sack. Then what? He could not shout for help for The Gang members would hear. Then he had an idea. On his hands and knees he crept up to the lounge door and peered in.

There seemed to be three of them – Wilf and two others. Wilf was holding a torch and the other two were trying to open a safe let into the wall. Gussie did not know it was a safe but he could hear what they whispered to each other. A rough voice growled:

"You never said that 'e kept the money in a safe, Wilf."

Wilf didn't sound his tough self at all, in fact he almost whined.

"I didn't know, did I?"

A third voice said:

"Better give it up. We 'aven't the tools to open that."

" 'Oo says we 'aven't?" the rough voice retorted. "I never bin beaten by a safe yet and this should be dead easy."

While they were talking Gussie had got to his feet. Very quietly he took the key out of the inside of the lounge door. Then softly he shut the door and locked it on the outside. Then he ran to the twins' wall and yelled:

"Help! Help! Thieves!"

He made such a noise that both twins woke up and shoved their heads out of their windows.

"Who is it?" Jonathan asked.

"It's me, Gussie. How is it when you need policemen? There are three thieves in the house."

It seemed no time after that before sirens were blowing and policemen all over the place. In most houses Wilf and his friends would have got away, but they did not know Cecil. The locks and chains on his front door were splendid, so Wilf and his friends were caught red-handed.

When the thieves, including a very cowed-looking Wilf, had been driven to the police station, the police sergeant who was in charge asked everybody to come into the lounge, including Mr Allan and the twins as well as Mabel, Francesco and Anna. By that time it was established that nothing had been stolen and no one had broken into the house.

"Now," said the police sergeant looking at Gussie, "you say you were in the garden. Had you left the French windows open?"

Gussie's thoughts were running around like a cage full of mice.

"Yes."

"So you let the thieves in. Did you do it on purpose?"

"No. I was tied in a sack."

"But what brought you down into the garden in the middle of the night?"

Gussie felt there was nothing for it but the truth.

"I was to paint a gnome blue."

"Disgraceful!" said Cecil.

"Paint a gnome blue!" The sergeant was puzzled. "I'm afraid you want a better story than that."

That annoyed Gussie.

"It's true. I was to paint a gnome blue."

The sergeant sounded very unbelieving.

"You were meeting the thieves to paint a gnome blue.

Then you know who they were."

Too clearly Gussie could hear Wilf making a gurgling sound and drawing his finger across his throat.

"Only one and I can't tell you his name."

Priscilla tried to help.

"We know one of them. He's Wilf who goes to our school."

In a very angry voice, Cecil said:

"I'm afraid you'll get no help from my nephew, Sergeant. Result of a bad upbringing."

None of the children was standing for that. Francesco said:

"No one shall say we had a bad upbringing. It was a beautiful upbringing before the earthquake."

"Beautiful," Anna agreed. "It is only now that Gussie does something bad – never before."

Gussie was furious.

"I don't see that I have done something bad now. It was me who got out of the sack and shouted to the twins to send for policemen, and it was me who managed to lock the thieves in. If I had not done that they would not have been caught."

The sergeant looked at the constable, who was taking notes.

"Take a torch and go out into the garden and see if you can find a sack and a length of rope."

While the constable was gone Mr Allan said:

"I must say, Sergeant, if what the boy says is true – and I

suspect it is – I should think he ought to get a reward. It was a stout effort getting that key out of the door, for if the thieves had caught him I hate to think what might have happened."

Before anyone could answer, and it was clear from the furious look on Cecil's face that he was going to, the constable was back with the sack and the rope.

"There," said Gussie, "you see, I was telling the truth."

Gussie looked almost fat with pride. It was more than Cecil could bear.

"If the sergeant has done with you, go up to bed, Augustus. I will deal with you in the morning."

"And you go too, dears," Mabel told Francesco and Anna. "I will be up with hot drinks for you all in a minute."

Cecil almost roared.

"Not for Augustus."

Then a very odd thing happened. Mabel, looking more than usually held together, this time by the sash of her shapeless dressing-gown, with her hair not falling down but meant to be down, puffed out:

"Augustus needs a hot drink more than the other two. He has been out in the night air in his dressing-gown, and he is certainly over-excited, which well he may be for, as Mr Allan said, he has been a very brave little boy. So if you will excuse us, Sergeant." Then, without looking at Cecil, she swept the children in front of her and marched out of the lounge.

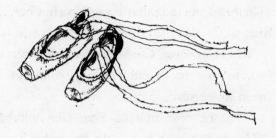

31. The Story Ends

EVEN IF YOU were up in the middle of the night rules were never changed in Dunroamin. So the children were called the same time as usual and were still half asleep when it was time to go down for breakfast.

Gussie was not feeling as pleased with himself as he had been during the night.

"Do you think," he whispered to Francesco, "that having meant to paint a gnome blue is enough for The Uncle to put me in a home?"

Francesco had no idea, but until S'William appeared he was still in charge.

"I do not think so. Anyway, if he does I will go too. I think Madame Scarletti will find room for Anna."

It was an even more awful breakfast than usual. If anyone had to speak it was in a whisper. Gussie afterwards said The

Uncle looked like a sky looks before there is thunder. And The Aunt, not as if a cat is catching her but as if it had caught her.

Breakfast over, Cecil made a pronouncement. "You will stay in your room this morning, Augustus. The police may need to see you."

On the way upstairs Francesco whispered to Gussie: "Thank goodness it is only you who has to stay in your room. I had thought it would be all of us so I was worried about Bessie and the hens."

"I thought of that too," Gussie agreed. "But I did not think he would lock our doors so we could have sneaked out."

Francesco looked sadly at Gussie. "That was a bad thought. Sometimes I think you will never learn how things are in Britain."

After Francesco and Anna had gone to the farm and Mabel had done the bedrooms, Gussie was very bored. He hung out of the window and thought about the excitement of last night and wondered how a gnome would look painted blue. Presently he heard the doorbell ring and guessed it was the police. He hoped they would send him for it would be something to do, but nothing happened. Then the front-door bell rang again. This time Gussie tiptoed into the passage to see who it was. Mabel, who had evidently been cooking, came along the passage drying her hands on her apron. She opened the door wide, but Gussie could not see who was there. Then a voice said:

"Good morning, Mrs Docksay."

Gussie made one rush and he was down the stairs clutching Sir William round the waist.

"Oh, it's so good you are home. Anna is needing to learn with that Madame Scarletti. Francesco is becoming like a cross old man and I may be sent to a home because I have trouble with thieves."

Sir William seemed never to change wherever he was. He had not now got Muzzaffer, the camel, on which he had arrived at Camp A. But otherwise he was exactly the same.

"I met Francesco and Anna at the end of the road. I have suggested we lunch together." He turned to Mabel. "I would like a few words with Mr Docksay if I might. Then, with his permission, I will take Gussie to join the others at a restaurant, they say it is called The Lotus Bud."

At The Lotus Bud Sir William, by refusing to allow more than one child to speak at a time, managed to get more or less the whole story of their stay in Dunroamin. At the end, he turned to Francesco.

"One way and another you seem to have managed well. Your uncle has agreed to the sale of your picture and in the meantime I will advance what is needed. I think you should buy a bicycle right away for Wally. It would be pleasant if it was waiting for him when he returns home."

To Anna he said:

"So you may become a great ballerina. Madame Scarletti spoke to me on the telephone last night. She will train you, and for the time being take you into her home. She has someone called Maria who will look after you."

Then he turned to Gussie.

"It was silly of you to want to paint your uncle's gnome blue, but I gather the police have decided that was your only crime. You know your uncle does not like children and you seem to have done nothing to make him change that opinion. What I would suggest is that I look around for a boarding school for you boys; there are some good ones about where you could both have fun as well as learn. But what we have to think about is the holidays, for Anna too will have holidays. Of course you could go to Dunroamin." The children groaned. "In fact, you must see your aunt, for she is very fond of you. Anyone got any ideas?"

It is strange how things happen. Where no ideas were before suddenly there was the same idea in all three children's heads.

"A caravan," said Francesco.

"Not one pulled by a horse like Togo," Gussie explained. "But one that stays where it is."

Anna nodded. "On Wally's dad's farm. There would perhaps be room for me in the house but not for the boys."

Sir William seemed pleased. He spoke in exactly the same voice as he used when he had stated: "The army say the runway will be open tomorrow, in which case we should get a plane for Istanbul." Now he said:

"Good. I will see Wally's dad as soon as he gets home. If he agrees, that sounds fine. Anyway, you can try things out, and if they don't work I shan't be far away. I'll keep in touch."

Francesco smiled at him.

"I hope you do. It is a great consolation to know where you are."

Postscript

It was in 1972 that my aunt Noel wrote *Ballet Shoes for Anna*, yet in one way it could have been the present day. As I write this afterword now, in 1998, there has again been an earthquake in Turkey, with over a hundred people killed and thousands injured – just such an earthquake that carried away Jardek, Babka, Christopher, Olga and Togo, together with their home and caravan. Noel herself had been in an earthquake, not in Turkey, but staying with friends in Rhodesia (now, of course, Zimbabwe); she noticed the effect – on the birds, particularly – then. Noel was a great noticer, and liked to experience events personally or have been in similar circumstances, or have seen people react when in similar circumstances, to be happy writing about them. Then her fertile imagination could do the rest.

A home destroyed by an earthquake is not greatly different from a home destroyed by a bomb. And Noel had seen plenty of that in the war when London was blitzed. People lost their families, homes and possessions, and were numbed with grief and shock just as were Francesco, Gussie and Anna. Noel had seen complete strangers come to the rescue and provide homes and hope, much as did her flamboyant S'William.

Before writing a book, Noel used to collect her ideas on pages of notes, and she reckoned to live with her characters for six to seven months before she even started to write. She used to say that if *she* didn't know her characters, her readers never would!

In *Ballet Shoes for Anna*, Noel was returning to her true

love – the ballet. Her first book for children, *Ballet Shoes*, she said she only wrote because it was a subject on which she doted. This passion for ballet and dancing started with her at the age of eleven when she stayed with relations who had taken a house at the then fashionable seaside resort of Hastings. Imagine her excitement at finding that in the house immediately opposite was a troupe of child dancers! Coming from the life of a vicarage – always to her unbearably restricted – the life of those children seemed unbelievable.

I remember visiting Noel about the time when she was writing *Ballet Shoes for Anna*. Her home was then near Eaton Square – at 51a Elizabeth Street – a smart area of London close to Victoria. Noel's flat was on the 3rd and 4th floors, and to reach it you had to climb a steep and rather dark staircase. There was a landing by the flat on the floor below Noel's, and it was surprising how often the owner popped out just as you were going past! I think she liked to know what was going on. Luckily, she and Noel were great friends.

The sitting room of the flat was large, with a beautiful carpet and curtains. Dominating the room was the lovely portrait by Lewis Baumer of Noel when she was about 30, with her auburn hair close-cropped. It now hangs in the National Portrait Gallery. On either side of this you could see out of large windows that looked across Elizabeth Street, with wooden window boxes on each sill. I remember them always to be full of wonderful flowers, because Noel was a great gardener. During the war she had even created her own garden in a space where houses once stood.

As you would expect, one wall was almost covered with a floor-to-ceiling bookcase, and behind the armchair where Noel usually sat was a splendid long mantelpiece with a fascinating array of little ornaments set along it, including a blue Dresden china clock in the centre. Into this striking room a small black poodle – whose name was Pierre – would usually make an appearance. He used to settle down by the armchair, and liked to accompany us if we all went out to dinner at Le Matelot – which was by extreme good fortune almost next door. He was always well looked after with scraps!

But of course Noel herself was the centre of our attention – she was such a larger-than-life character! Visiting her in the evening, particularly, was quite an experience. On arrival the drinks trolley was immediately wheeled in, and once everyone was settled down with the tipple of their liking, she would reach for her cigarettes. Those were the days when smoking was not only an acceptable part of everyday life, but it was then considered rude if you didn't have cigarettes in the house to offer your guests. Noel would produce her cigarette holder, the like of which I have never seen anywhere else, gold, and a ring to hold the cigarette on the end of a long stalk, with a ring at the other end which slipped round her finger to hold it. Noel smoked with a very distinctive puckering of the lips, and there she would sit, regaling us with her stories, or talking about the family. She was a great family person, and very interested in people.

Above all, Noel liked people with spirit. She had little time for wimps, or pompous people. If they were strong-willed and naughty, so much the better. She had been strong-willed and naughty as a child, and she discovered that readers liked the characters that were always in trouble, and children who were able to be a little bit more determined and brave than one would have been oneself in the same circumstances. So Gussie has us on tenterhooks as we wonder whether he will get into real trouble; the children make bold and self-sacrificing decisions to obtain, for them, apparently unattainable sums of money, and break out to impossibly inaccessible London for help. Cecil starts off a pompous ass, and remains one, but Mabel gives hope at the end that she will rise up and cease to be so feeble.

Ballet Shoes for Anna has many of the magic ingredients that Noel often wove through her books: a catastrophe that so shatters the children's world that they have to rely on each other to survive, (and we watch how the characters develop as the story unfolds); ballet as the central theme, with all the detail of the practice barre and the steps; and the emotionally charged moments when the grown-ups realise Anna's real talent, and finally come to the rescue. And Anna is not a heroine who just *likes* ballet – no. Anna is determined to succeed, and Francesco and Gussie are equally determined that she will be the best.

There were no half measures for Noel, and this determination to succeed against the odds, to shoot for the stars, is one of the qualities that have made her books dearly remembered favourites for many many years. More than one person has said to me that reading Noel's books in her childhood had created this feeling that anything is possible and you *could* change your life. I'm sure people said this to her also, but I know how happy she would be to hear that generation after generation of children is reading and enjoying her books, and getting from them pleasure and inspiration.

WILLIAM STREATFEILD

ELIDOR
BY ALAN GARNER

Four children from a Manchester suburb are drawn into Elidor, a twilight world almost destroyed by fear and darkness. And Elidor's salvation remains in the children's power alone. A richly imagined, spine-chilling book.

THE WEIRDSTONE OF BRISINGAMEN AND
THE MOON OF GOMRATH
BY ALAN GARNER

Fierce, wild fantasies about the loss and recovery of a stone containing great power and strength. In the highly evocative landscape of Cheshire, an area rich in legend, Susan and Colin are captured by evil forces in a struggle that leaves the reader spellbound and breathless.

THE OWL SERVICE
BY ALAN GARNER
(Winner of the Carnegie Medal and the Guardian Award)

Ancient jealousies, hatreds and high passions are re-awakened and lived anew by three young people who become trapped in a seemingly endless re-enactment of a tragic Welsh legend.

RED SHIFT
BY ALAN GARNER

Red Shift is a daring exploration of a contemporary love story cut into by two violent fragments from the past. The result is one of the most profoundly imaginative, strange, controversial, and rewardingly demanding novels to have been published for children.

THE CHRONICLES OF NARNIA

by C. S. LEWIS

C. S. Lewis's wit and wisdom, and his blend of excitement and adventure with fantasy, have made this magnificent series beloved of many generations of readers. The final book, *The Last Battle*, won the Carnegie Medal for 1956.

Each of the seven titles is a complete story in itself, but all take place in the magical land of Narnia. Guided by the noble Lion Aslan, the children learn that evil and treachery can only be overcome by courage, loyalty and great sacrifice.

The titles, in suggested reading order, are as follows:

Order Form

To order direct from the publishers, just make a list of the titles you want and fill in the form below:

Name ....

Address ....

....

....

Send to: Dept 6, HarperCollins Publishers Ltd, Westerhill Road, Bishopbriggs, Glasgow G64 2QT.

Please enclose a cheque or postal order to the value of the cover price, plus:

UK & BFPO: Add £1.00 for the first book, and 25p per copy for each additional book ordered.

Overseas and Eire: Add £2.95 service charge. Books will be sent by surface mail but quotes for airmail despatch will be given on request.

A 24-hour telephone ordering service is available to holders of Visa, MasterCard, Amex or Switch cards on 0141- 772 2281.

Collins
An *Imprint* of HarperCollins*Publishers*